1

'All life fears time, but time fears the Pyramids,' quoted Amber Davis as she peered out of the carriage window at Cairo's poverty-bitten suburbs.

'Indeed,' murmured her father. As usual, Professor Oliver Davis had his head in a book. This time, unsurprisingly, it was a book on ancient Egypt. The professor was a renowned Egyptologist who had passed his love of all things Egyptian to his pretty twenty-two-year-old daughter.

'Imagine, Laura,' Amber said, turning to her maid, who was fanning herself in the heat, 'here at last!'

'You really should close the blinds, miss.' Laura sighed. 'You'll get brown as a nut, and freckled, and your eyes will line with squinting.'

It was a happy circumstance that Amber had a maid older than herself.

Usually ladies' maids were younger or the same age as their mistresses, but her father had deemed it prudent to employ a more mature woman.

Amber secretly felt that he had been trying to find a substitute for her mother. Although nothing could ever replace a mother's arms, Laura had been a comfort and a wise guide. In all respects, if Amber had ever had a mother, it was the loyal Laura.

'Oh, don't fuss so.' Amber pressed her face to the window of the conveyance. 'How should I see then? I want to see everything.'

They rolled on. The journey had been long: two weeks by sea to Alexandria and then by train to Cairo. Now they were travelling to the villa of Mr Lachlan Hayes, hotel magnate and the richest ex-patriot in Egypt. But the voyage had not fatigued Amber. She was simply too excited.

'Have you ever met Mr Hayes, Father?' Amber asked, unfastening the top button of her blouse and pushing a

GIFT OF THE NILE

Amber Davis has always loved hearing about her father's archaeological excavations, and is thrilled when she is finally allowed to accompany the professor on an expedition. As she begins her Egyptian adventure, she meets expatriates Lachlan and his son James. Amber is drawn to the artistic and bohemian James, but is concerned about the lecherous eye of his father. When things begin to go very wrong during the trip, can Amber keep her head . . . and her heart?

HEIDI SULLIVAN

---◆---

GIFT OF
THE NILE

Complete and Unabridged

LINFORD
Leicester

First published in Great Britain in 2016

First Linford Edition
published 2017

A catalogue record for this book is available
from the British Library.

ISBN 978–1–4448–3366–9

Published by
F. A. Thorpe (Publishing)
Anstey, Leicestershire

Set by Words & Graphics Ltd.
Anstey, Leicestershire
Printed and bound in Great Britain by
T. J. International Ltd., Padstow, Cornwall

This book is printed on acid-free paper

twist of hair, the lustre of polished mahogany, away from her face.

'Oh, about two years ago, if I recall correctly.' Professor Davis folded down a corner of his book to mark the page and looked over the top of his gold-rimmed spectacles at his daughter. 'It must have been. Yes, 1890 it was. I remember now; I had just come back from the excavation in Karnak.'

'Oh, yes.' Amber nodded and settled back.

'His villa is on the east bank of the Nile, and I believe it's extremely opulent. I stayed in one of his hotels. Beautiful, it was. It seems he wishes to build yet another in Luxor, but he's found what appears to be a burial site, and wishes me to look at it. The work has stopped for the moment, and he's anxious to discover whether the site is important or not. If not, we will simply clear the remaining artefacts and let them build. If it *is* important, we'll need to look into it; have a full archaeological excavation.'

'Wouldn't that make Mr Hayes cross, sir?' Laura asked. She was used to joining in conversations between the professor and his daughter. Amber was pleased. It showed that Laura felt she fitted in and was part of the family.

'It would cost him money, yes.' Professor Davis frowned. 'I don't know whether to hope it's a burial site or not.'

'I'm just glad you let us join you,' Amber said. 'I've heard you talk about Egypt so much, it's truly wonderful to be here at last.'

Her father smiled and patted her hand indulgently. 'Yes, my dear. I'm glad I brought you, despite the fact that I know you will be a minx and want to get involved in the excavation, if there is one.' With that, he opened his book and returned to the page he was reading.

Amber and Laura contented themselves with looking out onto Cairo. It seemed rather dangerous and uncoordinated. In a lot of ways it was a normal city, until a statue emerged here and there from the sandy dust. It was a strange mixture of modern and ancient, and Amber could see why her father loved this country.

She had been captivated from the minute she landed in Alexandria. Even the air was strange. If felt different and smelt different: warm and still. She had been a little dazed by it all and had clung to Laura as her father negotiated their passage to the train station, chatting in fluent Arabic and bustling through until they finally boarded the train to Cairo.

Her father shouting 'Stop!' suddenly threw her back from her reverie. Laura squealed and grabbed at the hand strap hung for the purpose of steadying passengers. Used to her father's erratic behaviour, Amber simply peered out in an effort to see what had caused Professor Davis to exclaim so.

'Come with me.' Davis alighted and strode purposefully towards a gate leading, it seemed, to a back yard. Amber leapt down, followed by her maid.

'You really should let me help you, miss,' Laura scolded.

'Tish,' Amber scoffed. 'What is it, Father?' She followed him and gasped.

'There are your Pyramids, my dear.'

The block-on-block man-made mountains loomed black against the sky over the mundane brick wall. A bitter disappointment stung Amber. She had not expected her first sight of these fearful wonders to be from the shabby back yard of a southern suburb of Cairo.

'They're very big, sir.' Laura shielded her eyes and stared up at the pyramids. 'But I had rather expected to see them in the desert or some such.'

'Well, this is the first view one gets, made all the more poignant when seen against poverty.'

'Rather like seeing the Tower of London from the East End,' mused Amber.

'Quite. Past glories vying with present inequality.' Davis turned to his daughter. 'If we are to reach this villa, we must move on. I'm beginning to get hungry.'

The trio returned to their carriage and reboarded. The sun was now so hot that even Amber had to admit they must draw the blinds. Laura did so with a sigh of relief.

★   ★   ★

'Ah, Davis!' Lachlan Hayes boomed. 'This must be your lovely daughter, Amber.' He took Amber's small hand and kissed it. His lips felt powder-dry and cool on her warm skin. It set her flesh crawling unaccountably. She shivered in spite of the heat.

'Yes, and this is Laura — Miss Dobson. Here to keep my lamb out of mischief, and a Godsend for that.' Davis laughed, and Amber saw his expressive brown eyes fill with love for her. He had brought her up single-handedly from the age of two. Her mother had died of childbed fever, giving birth to a stillborn son. Amber and her father had cleaved together, so close that paper could not pass between them.

'And a trial she is too, sir.' Laura laughed with him.

Hayes still held Amber's fingers, his eyes travelling over her slender frame; the look on his face giving her, alarmingly, the impression of a hungry wolf. Her father had not seemed to notice, but the ever-vigilant Laura had. She cleared her throat and said, 'Mr Hayes, I am sure you will not think it impertinent if I request that my mistress freshens up. The journey was terribly long, and I fear that she feels a little travel-worn.'

Hayes snatched back his fingers as if they had been burnt. 'Indeed.' He inclined his head. 'Please do. I shall have a servant show you to your room, Miss Davis. It is quite comfortable.'

Laura pressed her fingers into Amber's shoulder to steer her from the libidinous Hayes, who was watching as Amber made her way upstairs, following the bird-like maid.

When they were alone in the room, Laura sniffed in derision. 'I don't care much for Mr Hayes. Quite ungentlemanly, unlike your father. Professor Davis is a paragon when next to him.'

'Oh Laura, I expect he was trying to be kind.' But Amber shuddered at the memory of Hayes's touch.

Laura helped Amber to change. She was expert at the fiddly hook-and-eye fastenings of the dresses and the slithery laces of corsets. She eased Amber into a dress of tawny silk, its skirts whispering as she arranged the folds and smoothed out creases. She piled the heavy red-brown curls on to Amber's head and stood back in satisfaction as soft twists frothed around the heart-shaped face.

'There,' she said, picking a speck off the yellow skirt. 'Lovely.'

Amber turned so she could see her whole reflection. The dress nipped in neatly at her tiny waist and fell fashionably close to her slim hips. A necklace of amber chunks sat trim in the hollow of her throat, burnished and smooth against the cream of her skin. Her father had given it to her for her twenty-first birthday. From her ears hung yellow drops of the jewel, her namesake. She was satisfied with the result.

'Now, we go to dinner with the 'wonderful' Lachlan Hayes.' She grinned at her maid. 'Still, we're in Egypt, and nothing else matters.'

They made their way down to dinner. The room was gaudy and ostentatious, set out in maroon velvet and green leather. A butler stood tall and stiff as a tree next to the tiny maid who had earlier shown her to her room. Amber and Laura were the first to arrive.

'Please take a seat, Miss Davis, Miss Dobson.' The butler pulled out their chairs; winged chairs of the same solid oak as the table. 'Mr Hayes and Professor Davis will join you shortly, ma'am. Can I offer you a drink?'

Amber said she would like a little

watered wine and Laura accepted the same. They were just about to take their first sips when Hayes and Amber's father came into the room, laughing heartily.

'Amber, my dear, you beat us to it.' Davis sat down and rubbed his hands. 'Now then, what do you say? We are to have clear soup, lobster and partridges. All imported, my dear. And caramel pudding to finish.'

'I hope you realise that the soup is turtle, and not mock either.' Hayes took a deep gulp of his wine. 'And I could simply not offer you just mutton, now could I? Although my cook makes a remarkable roast with artichokes.'

'My daughter adores lobster, don't you, my darling?'

Amber nodded, aware of Hayes's eyes locked onto her.

'Now, Davis, my little discovery in Luxor. What do you make of it, eh?'

'From what you say and from the artefacts you've just shown me, I would be inclined to be excited about it, sir. I

11

think you have a very important find. I think it's the site of a royal burial. Unusual for it to be outside the Valley of the Kings or the Valley of the Queens. That's what makes it so interesting. I shall hardly sleep tonight for wanting to see it.'

Hayes's face had fallen. 'You think it important, then?'

'Indeed I do. Yes, a most intriguing find.'

Amber looked worriedly at her maid. She knew that Hayes stood to lose the money he had already invested in the site. Would he be angry with her father for putting a stop to the building of his hotel? By the look on her host's face, it seemed more than likely.

The door to the villa's dining room opening interrupted her nervous thoughts. She was startled to see an ash-blond young man with eyes the colour of smoke enter the room. Smiling brightly, he sat down and grinned at the assembled party.

'Well, what a feast,' he said. 'Lobster, I hear.'

Amber felt her heart flutter like a pet bird in a cage. He was incredibly handsome. His eyes alighted on her for a few delicious moments. He smiled, but then looked across at her father. 'Professor Davis,' he said, 'I've been so long looking forward to meeting you. I read your book about Karnak. I found it grand.'

Laura was looking at Amber, a strange and unreadable expression on her soft features. Amber twisted the delicate stem of her wineglass in her slim fingers All of a sudden she felt gauche and clumsy. Her frame, slender as it was, seemed too tall; and her hair, although arranged fashionably, seemed untidy, with tendrils falling around her face like curl papers.

'My son, James.' Hayes took a sharp breath. 'Another trial, I'm afraid, Miss Dobson.'

Laura lowed her lashes demurely. 'I'm not sure, sir.'

'He wishes be a writer. A writer of novels and even poems.' Lachlan Hayes harrumphed in derision. 'He has the whole of my hotel empire to come when I leave this mortal coil, and yet he spends precious time scribbling.'

'I should imagine, though, that you're proud of such an imaginative and creative son,' Amber said, diplomatic to the last.

'Proud? Ha! I want a businessman as a son, not a flimsy poet.' Hayes shook his greying head. 'I'll not have it. It won't do, sir.' He turned now to his handsome son. 'Indeed, it will not.'

James shook his head and leant forward on his elbow. 'Writing is like breathing to me, Father. I cannot live without it. Besides, I'll be thirty in June. You have very little say, I'm afraid. Anyway, when I pen my first masterpiece, I shall dedicate it to you: '*To Lachlan Sholto Hayes, sceptic.*''

Amber laughed, and then checked herself when Lachlan's eyes turned to her. He said: 'I imagine you think it romantic, Byronic even, to write such twaddle? You're young, Miss Davis. You are a girl. I don't expect you to understand that money turns this world, not flowery words.'

'The pen is mightier than the sword,' James said, smiling at Amber. 'Is it not, Miss Davis?'

Amber was mortified to find herself under James's scrutiny. Her cheeks, she knew, must be pink, for they were certainly hot. She could think of nothing to say in answer.

'Ha! Will a pen buy a villa such as this?' boomed Lachlan.

'If one becomes famous for his works of prose, then yes.' James was obviously beginning to warm to what Amber imagined to be a soapbox subject.

'Well, you will soon learn when you're starving in a garret somewhere.'

Hayes sat back as the meal was brought in. Silver platters were laid before them. The smell of food was so inviting that the party set to, the only sounds being the clink of silver on china and the sipping of good wine.

Amber took the opportunity to watch James more closely. He was bent to his meal, enjoying it heartily. He was bright and cheerful, giving her the feeling that he had just gulped a lungful of fresh air. He was certainly handsome. She ignored her heart's fluttering. He was a rich man's son; she was the daughter of a widowed professor. People such as Lachlan Hayes arranged elegant and haughty heiresses for their sons, not flighty, wilful mares such as she.

Eventually, conversation was started again by James asking her father about the find at Luxor. Davis explained his theories and James listed with rapt attention. Amber usually loved to hear her father speak of ancient history, but now she could not concentrate on what he was saying. He mind was too set on James. She drank in the way his shoulder muscles knotted as he leaned forward to hear her father the better. She watched as his deep eyes widened at some intriguing fact.

Foolish! she scolded herself. Her fancies would overtake her, Laura had always said. She was in Egypt to take in its culture and, hopefully, to help with her father's excavation. She had no time for romance. She was far too interested in the adventure for such giddiness. But as she watched James Hayes for a little longer, she began to realise that stirring deep within her was a disturbing and new sensation. James's grey eyes and smile sent her as weak as a kitten.

2

Amber's excitement at the prospect of seeing Luxor for the first time was tempered by the fact that James would be joining the excursion. She had hoped to leave him behind in Cairo, so as to ignore the painful beating of her heart every time he was near her. He seemed totally unmoved by her presence, and this made her feel young and ridiculous.

'So, Miss Davis, we shall be exploring the delights of Luxor together, eh?' James had met her in the garden as she sat in the shade of a banana tree. She took her book away from her face and frowned into the sun at him.

'So it would seem, Mr Hayes.'

'Now, I was wondering — if we are to be companions on this trip, why not at least agree to first-name terms?'

Amber pursed her full pink lips. 'I could not, sir.'

James threw back his blond head and laughed. 'Oh, my dear Miss Davis, I believe you can. Don't, please, stand on ceremony with me, for I shan't with you. I never do. Hang it all! We shall, I assume, become friends, and so must be willing to address each other as such, Amber. A jewel, all golden brown.' He sat beside her. 'And me? James. Plain James, I fear. I should have preferred Sebastian or Henriques. More fitting for a writer, don't you think?'

'You take your writing seriously, Mr Hayes.'

'James, or I shall wail a thousand laments to the gods.'

Amber laughed and nodded. 'I should hate you to deafen Horus, so I shall agree to James.'

'That's settled, then.' He gave her his shining grin.

'I wish you well and look forward to seeing your finished works displayed in the best bookshops.'

'You mock me, Amber?' He had become solemn, the wide smile vanishing from his face.

'Oh no!' She sat up then, anxious to relieve him of his misinterpretation. 'I don't mock you at all. I genuinely wish you well.'

His face broke out once again into his wonderful smile. 'Then I'm grateful to you for being the one person on this planet to believe in me.'

She laughed, basking happily in his warmth. Her reservations and worries about him joining them on their trip to the proposed hotel site melted, and she found herself chatting easily with him. Until Laura came out into the garden.

'Miss Amber.'

Amber had been leaning into James, their faces almost touching as they joked and twitted each other like old friends. She now leapt back like a cat on hot coals. James stood up and bowed slightly in greeting to Laura. But Laura's ruffled feathers and fierce protection of her ward would not allow her to be softened by his charm. She stood purposefully next to Amber.

'I worry about you, miss. Please come inside. I don't wish you to get burnt.'

Amber knew that her maid and companion was not concerned about the hot Cairo sun. She stood up with a sigh. 'You're right, Laura. I may get burnt easily if I stay out too long.'

James looked strangely at her. 'I assure you, my dear Amber, I would never allow you to burn.' His voice was as soft as a summer breeze. 'Please rest assured that in my company no harm will ever come to you.'

Laura took Amber's elbow and steered her forcefully inside the villa. When they reached Amber's guest-room, Laura turned to her with concern in her green eyes.

'Miss Amber, I beg you not to be alone with Mr Hayes. It is unseemly for a young lady to speak with a young gentleman without an appropriate chaperone. You really must remember that. But — ' Here she smoothed away a stray twist of hair from Amber's cheek. ' — you are young. Perhaps you didn't realise.'

But Amber did realise. She understood vaguely the hammering of her heart in her breast. She knew full well why her mouth turned dry as dust whenever she thought of James. Laura fancied Amber to be an innocent child. But she was twenty-two, and was blossoming into a woman.

★　★　★

'Now Amber, my darling, what do you remember of Luxor?' Professor Davis pushed his spectacles up onto the bridge of his nose and watched as Amber played with a rail-thin stray kitten that had wandered into the garden.

Amber looked up from where she was tickling the painfully emaciated cat. 'Well, it has a lively bazaar, from what I remember you telling me.'

'Come now, I told you more than that. If you're to help in this excavation, I'd like to know what you remember.'

'It grew up to the south of the old Egyptian capital of Thebes — on the south of the canal, while Karnak grew to the north. The temple there is known as Amon's Southern Harem by locals.' She twitched her mouth into a smile as Davis flustered a little.

'Well yes, but you need not really know about such things. The important fact is that it was a most significant place to the ancients, and as such, this site of Hayes could be very important. Over a third of the world's greatest antiquities come from Luxor.'

'I can't wait to see it.'

They were to travel on Lachlan Hayes's *dahabeeya* — his luxury barge. The cruise up the Nile would be leisurely and gentle. When Amber saw the vessel for the first time, she was wonderfully surprised at how opulent it was. Moored on the banks of the river, nestled amongst the fringes of green foliage, it gleamed bright white in the sun.

'Welcome to the *Amethyst Sea*,' James said, his hair burnished by the climate and his eyes seeming almost blue in the haze of the heat and water's reflection. 'I'd give anything to live on her, watching the Nile banks pass by. It's like a child's storybook, Amber.'

He wore aesthete dress — knee breeches of saffron-coloured kid, a shirt the bright colour of poppies, and a flowing tie the same hue as his breeches. Amber felt itchy and hot in her corset of steel and whalebone; and although her pale teal dress was of cool cotton, she would have preferred the outfit worn by James, for it seemed much more comfortable.

They had come down to the boat before anyone else. Laura had been repacking Amber's linen for the journey, and James had boldly asked Amber to come down to the little dock to see the *dahabeeya* while her faithful maid was busy. Amber had been shocked at his audacity.

'Oh Amber, come on,' he had beseeched. 'I won't bite, and our fathers and Laura will be down soon enough.'

'Then I shall go with them,' she had replied, rather more haughtily than she had wanted to.

'I suppose you think me terribly forward.' James had looked crestfallen. 'But you seem such an unconventional girl that I felt you wouldn't mind.'

Calling her unconventional was a compliment. Amber looked through her long lashes and gave a reluctant smile. 'I shall come with you, but only for a short time. Laura will have the vapours as it is.'

Now as they stood, dazzled by the boat's reflection of the sun, Amber was actually glad that she had come.

'You, sir — James!'

She was startled by the strident voice of Lachlan Hayes.

'What the devil are you doing?'

James pushed back his shoulders. 'I was showing Amb — Miss Davis the

Amethyst, Father.'

'Alone?' Hayes frowned down at his son. 'By any standards, even your own regrettably low ones, that is unacceptable.'

'My standards are not low,' bristled James. 'And we were expecting you and Professor Davis at any minute. We were not alone long, I can assure you on that point.'

'Long enough,' muttered his father. He pulled at his whiskers and turned to Amber. 'You must forgive my son his uncouth manners. I really cannot see what he hoped to achieve by compromising you in such a fashion.'

'Really, Mr Hayes, I wasn't — ' Amber was interrupted by the sight of Laura hurrying down to the water's edge, holding on to her straw hat and looking flustered and piqued.

'Oh, miss!' She stood breathlessly. 'I was worried sick.'

'Sorry, Laura, but Mr Hayes asked me to join him. He wished to show me his *dahabeeya*.'

'Mmm.' Laura looked pointedly at James. 'Indeed.'

'The boat,' explained James with a laugh.

'I have the *boab* bringing the luggage. We can, I believe, board now,' Lachlan announced, glaring for one last time at his son before boarding the vessel.

Amber caught James's gaze once more. Despite her reservations, she felt that the time on this boat in his company might not be so bad after all.

As the party boarded, Amber looked around in wonder at the elegant furnishings. The salon boasted a piano and plush velvet seats, and the upper deck was charmingly laid out as an outdoor room, with fragile, delicate furniture.

'What do you make of this tub and bucket, eh, Miss Davis?' Lachlan Hayes beamed round proudly at his guests.

'It's more wonderful than I had imagined.'

'Good.' He rubbed plump hands

together. 'We shall soon be on our way.'

While the crew was preparing to sail, Amber took the opportunity to peruse her quarters. She and Laura had a sitting room and bedroom. The sitting room had a davenport desk, its top gently sloping, balloon-backed and inlaid with a mother-of-pearl floral design on gleaming black, and Japanned papier-mâché chairs. The bedroom was small but very comfortable. The bedstead carried the same design as the sitting room furniture, and there was even a very ornate dressing table, its mirror secured to gilded scrollwork.

There was a tap on the door. Laura answered and saw Professor Davis.

'Ah, Amber my dear. I came to tell you that lunch will be served on the upper deck. You'll need your sunbonnet.'

Laura began to fuss with the bags, trying to locate the hat.

'How do you like your cabin then, Amber?' Davis continued. 'Mine is wonderful. It even has an oak writing desk. I shall begin my new book by writing about this expedition.'

Amber laughed. 'Will you never see this as a holiday?'

'No, not when I am to see what I suspect to be the tomb of Princess Amratep.'

Amber's mouth fell open and she stared at her father. 'But you've been looking for that for twenty years!'

'Yes, and now I may have found it. Hayes showed me a portion of a pot from the hotel site with an inscription carved into the clay on the underside. It is not all there, but there's a cartouche which I am certain gives the name Amratep.'

Amber looked at her father's shining eyes. Ever since he had read of the legend of the beautiful princess who had tragically killed herself when her lover proved to be untrue, he had wanted to prove she existed. She had been next in line to a pharaoh of the twelfth dynasty, but her death had supposedly skewed the line of succession. If he had really found the tomb, then history would have to be rewritten. He would be very, very famous.

'I am sure it's Amratep's tomb, hidden all these years just beneath the sand and dust.' Davis took a deep breath. 'And you shall be there to see it excavated.'

★   ★   ★

The sailors had put up awnings on the upper deck, shielding the party from the sun. A lunch of tomato soup and mushrooms on toast was to be served, and the table was laid ready with crisp white cloths. Amber wandered up to the deck, her parasol shading her porcelain skin. She was alone, looking out at the river. The Nile swelled a little here, its banks lush and fertile as they had been for countless millennia. She watched two goats gambol at the edge and listened to the sailors shouting curses and orders in their musical Arabic tongue. Soon they would move off from the dock and begin the slow journey up the great river.

'Thinking of the soup?'

Amber started. James had come to join her, holding on to the rail as she was doing, and squinting out at the river. A brown-as-a-berry boy came paddling past in a tin bucket.

'*Salaam*,' said the imp, his grin as bright as the *Amethyst Sea*.

James waved. '*Salaam alaykum. Ez zayak?*'

'*Kua yiss.*' The boy turned to Amber. '*Enti Gamela.*'

'*Shukran!*' James tipped his trilby and laughed as the boy waved and paddled away.

Amber frowned. 'What was that all about?'

'He said hello, I asked how he was, he said you were pretty, and I thanked him on your behalf.'

Amber felt her cheeks heat. 'Impertinent puppy.'

'He was only a child.'

31

'I wasn't talking about the boy.' She pursed her lips at him, but knew that the corners of her mouth tilted upwards. 'James, I think you're impertinent and brazen. Here we are alone again, and I'm surprised at your talk.'

'Rubbish!' James snapped. 'You are not one to allow small-minded men like my father to wedge their way into a friendship. Good lord, woman! I can and will say you're pretty, whether you think it rude or not. You are, Miss Davis the most *gamela* woman I know — and to the dogs with anyone who says I can't speak it!'

Amber had decided not to speak. Her head was in a whirl. Why was he doing this? Why did he deliberately ask her to flout convention? She badly wanted to be alone with him and laugh with him. But her father was on the same boat, and she did not want him to think badly of her. Also — and this was surely the most painful admission — she did not want the professor to feel that she would leave him. She loved her father, and falling in love would take her from him. She did not want to leave him alone in the world. As clever and educated as he was, he was emotionally vulnerable.

All things considered, getting involved with James was only going to lead to heartache. As Amber watched him stamp off, affronted, she sighed and gripped the boat's rail. Now the trip to Luxor would be agony for her bruising heart.

3

The light lunch was a torment to Amber. No one seemed to notice the tension between herself and James. At first he spoke only a few curt words to her, and she spent the first few minutes of the meal avoiding those grey eyes. Her mind fluttered over the events of a quarter of an hour before, and she was struck by how suddenly their budding friendship had been clipped.

'So, Miss Davis, how are you enjoying your trip?' Lachlan Hayes was spooning soup noisily into his wide, fleshy mouth.

Amber managed a weak smile. 'Very well, sir. Thank you so much for inviting us.'

Her host grinned through a mouthful of light, airy Egyptian bread. 'Good, good.'

James looked intently at her. 'Do you

not feel a little constrained?'

'I beg your pardon?'

'I get the impression that you want to spread your wings, but feel too restricted.'

Amber bristled. She could sense a challenge, even an insult behind those words, and it was most certainly unworthy of James to be so sly. 'I'm sorry, Mr Hayes, but I cannot grasp your meaning. If you refer to our conversation earlier, then I can assure you I have no constraints.'

'What's this?' Lachlan frowned at his son. 'What conversation is this?'

'We were discussing . . . ' Here James smiled lopsidedly at Amber. 'What were we discussing, Miss Davis?'

'I believe we were discussing some rather impertinent comments. I understood those observations to be impudent and a little fresh.' She held his gaze.

'Ah, but true. Fresh they may well have been, but I believe those sentiments to be sincere.'

'Impudent comments?' Laura looked up from her plate. 'What comments, Miss Amber?' She turned sharp, motherly eyes to James.

'Some boy passed by in a bucket and told me, in Arabic, that your dear mistress was pretty. And I, in my wisdom, declared that it was quite a valid assertion.'

Laura's cheeks grew little hot patches of colour. 'Goodness me! How coarse, that child!'

'Miss Dobson,' soothed James, 'he was a young boy, and we can't escape the fact that Miss Davis is very lovely.' James lowered his eyes, but then peeked over at Amber with such a wicked grin that she could not help but let the corners of her own mouth twitch up.

'That's better, my dear Miss Davis. Such a lovely smile should not be hidden in the shadow of a frown.'

'James!' snapped his father. 'How dare you talk so freely with the young lady? Sir, I command that you apologise for your vulgarity this moment.'

James shook his head as if in wonder at his father's silliness. 'Oh, every young lady likes compliments. Really, you can be very starched and uppity.'

Lachlan's face turned a violent shade of puce. 'James!'

'Please,' begged Amber. 'I'm sorry to have caused such upset, but really, the comments were nothing.'

Lachlan's colour paled back to normal and he sniffed. 'Well, your diplomacy does you credit, Miss Davis. I only hope James hasn't upset you. I would see him horsewhipped before he offended so delicate a flower as yourself.'

Laura hissed a breath and shot a look at the turned head of Lachlan. Amber pressed her maid's fingers briefly. 'I'm fine,' she said to assure both Hayes and Laura. 'James did not cause me any upset. Quite the reverse.'

For all of this time, Amber's own father had been quietly listening to the heated voices. Now he put down his cutlery very deliberately and said: 'I am sure that if my daughter was offended, she would have said so.'

'Indeed,' said James heartily.

★　★　★

'We shall soon be passing through the eastern desert,' Professor Davis told Amber as she sipped a coolly refreshing peppermint cordial. They were sitting on the upper deck of the *dahabeeya*, under the shade of a wide gazebo. Amber shielded her large brown eyes and looked over the water.

'There are quite a few rock tombs scattered about,' Davis continued, 'and I have a feeling that Amratep's tomb, if that is indeed what Hayes has found, may be connected to them.'

Amber considered this. 'Surely if it's a burial site of a princess, that is unusual. I thought royalty were buried in the valleys, like the Valley of the Queens.'

'There must be some reason why Amratep's tomb hasn't been found there. Indeed, it may still be that she's a myth. However, I don't believe so. Bodies were often taken to secret burials because of thieves and tomb robbers. Also, tombs were placed on top of one another or dug deep into the rocks or ground. It may simply be that no one has discovered anything solid about her existence.'

Amber took another sip of her drink and sat back to enjoy another history lesson from her father. He talked of two rival dynasties overlapping; of Nubian armies usurping the Pharaohs and mixing with the Egyptians to eventually rule. Amratep, according to legend, had been part Nubian, part Egyptian; the daughter of a pharaoh and one of his consorts.

Davis was just telling Amber about the high priest, once an army officer from the north with whom the princess had fallen in love, when the baize door to the deck opened and James entered. Davis stopped and stood to greet him.

James inclined his head in greeting

and said hello to Amber very softly. 'I hope I'm not interrupting anything, sir,' he said, hovering uneasily. 'Please tell me if I am and I shall leave.'

'Oh, Mr Hayes, I can assure you that you're not interrupting at all. In fact, please sit down and listen.'

James settled back into one of the comfortable seats. 'What are we listening to?'

'A story of tragic love,' Amber said. She watched his eyes, then pulled herself back to listening to her father.

'Priests were very influential,' the professor was saying. 'They were of the highest class. Amratep would have seen Ankhra quite often, no doubt as an advisor to her father.'

'Ankhra being the priest she fell in love with?' James asked.

Amber took over her father's tale. 'So when he supposedly absconded with the money, incense and other things left at the temple as offerings, the princess was distraught. She had imagined him to be true, but then it seemed as if she had been wrong. She took her own life.'

'So she was misled,' James said. 'I see. If Ankhra had truly loved the princess, then he would not have let her down by stealing.'

'I think that worse than being a thief was the fact that he was a liar.' Amber twisted her powder-blue skirt in her small hands, watching the material crimp into folds.

'So you think that being honest about your emotions is more important than being honest about material possessions?'

At first, Amber thought James was mocking her. Either that, or challenging what he assumed to be a silly, girlish ideal. She looked at him sharply, spots of colour staining her high cheekbones. About to retort indignantly, she noticed the serious look in his smoky eyes. Before showing herself up as snappish and too quick-tongued, she bit back the comment. Her reply stumbled. 'I, well . . . perhaps.'

'Yes, Miss Davis?' James leant forward, elbows on knees. He was, Amber realised with a bird-like flutter of her heart, genuinely interested in her views.

'Of course honesty is important. But my point is that being honest about what you feel is as important as not stealing. Amratep must have been devastated by Ankhra suddenly taking away his love for her.'

'Perhaps she had invested her emotions too heavily,' said James. 'It may not be wise to invest all your hopes and dreams in one person.'

'But isn't that just what love is all about?' Amber was becoming animated. 'Surely love is just that.'

James nodded. 'Of course it is. I never said it wasn't. I simply asked if it was wise.'

Amber shook her glossy curls in exasperation. 'But is that really what matters — being wise? Love is not like that at all. It's meant to be wild and free. It shouldn't be some staid or planned thing. Men are so mechanical.'

Davis laughed. 'Indeed we are, my dear. But Mr Hayes has a point. Is it really a good idea to rush headlong into something when it could save heartache to be more measured about it?'

Amber sat back in her chair. 'When I fall in love, I want it to be as if I could do nothing else. I don't want it to be measured. I want to *fall* in love, not walk in with a map and compass.'

James smiled at her and said softly, 'You may be wiser than you think, Miss Amber Davis.'

4

The *Amethyst Sea* was to pull to a stop on the west bank. They had passed the marshland of the northern delta and had lost sight of the rocky mountains that hemmed the valley. The flood waters were already beginning to swell the Nile, and the flora and fauna were rich.

The boat moored and the party disembarked. They had decided to go to the eastern bank in order for the professor to study the *mastabas* there. Amber recalled that *mastabas* were burial chambers used for higher-ranking Egyptians such as those at the royal court or the nobles. She was excited about seeing them, and she had even placed a small notebook of hieroglyphics in her handbag in order to try and help her father decipher the ancient picture writing.

'Miss Amber, please don't forget your bonnet. And take your shawl. The sun will be blazing,' Laura lectured, fussing about. Once Amber was hatted and shawled to her maid's satisfaction, the party was ready to board another small boat.

Amber looked over at James as he took over the manning of the little boat. He had rolled up his shirt sleeves, and Amber felt her insides tumble as she watched his strong arms pull effortlessly at the ropes and rudder. He turned then, catching her off guard.

'Miss Davis, would you like to help?' he asked.

Delighted, Amber leapt up. James helped and guided her in her tentative first attempts at sailing the small vessel. He came up behind her, his hands above hers on a rope. Together they took the little boat to the shore and the party disembarked.

'Your carriage awaits,' James said, laughing at Laura's horrified expression. A group of bored-looking camels stood waiting, held by their reins by an equally bored-looking keeper.

The group mounted the camels, and Amber giggled as her own camel wobbled up onto its feet and began to sway forward. After assuring herself that Laura was beginning to cope with her first-ever camel ride, she grabbed the chance to catch up with James, who was happily riding at the front of the group.

'You seem quite happy on humps,' she said, drawing level with him.

'I love camel riding. I have my own.'

'No! You're teasing me.'

'I'm not. His name is Cedric.' James patted the brown neck of his mount. 'Say hello now, then. Cedric, this is Amber, but you must call her Miss Davis when in polite company.'

Amber's face fell. 'You're teasing me again.'

'No, but I do wish that I could call you by your first name when we're in company. I hate being friends only when we're alone. It would be so pleasant to be relaxed with you all the time.'

'We're hardly ever alone though, James.'

'Well, Amber, I will endeavour to make as many attempts as I can at being alone with you. I'm a man of the deepest honour, but I cannot abide the idea of not being able to have a decent conversation with you without needing someone to look over our shoulders.'

'You want to shock me. Trying to be alone with me! That's preposterous.'

James simply watched her for a little, then said: 'So, are you suitably scandalised by me yet?'

'I can only imagine that you're a merciless and cruel man when it comes to my sensitivities.' She sniffed haughtily.

'Being chaperoned does not make it easy for a man to be honest. I am a writer of fiction, Amber, and used to creating characters. You could say that makes me a little bit of an actor in some ways.'

She was now completely lost. She frowned at him in incomprehension.

'You don't understand my meaning, do you?'

'I confess I'm a little bewildered by what you're saying, yes.'

'Then wait till I get you alone, Amber Davis,' James said, 'and I'll explain my cryptic message to you. But here's a clue to what I wish to say. Ankhra may not have been able to be honest with the princess because of her expectations of him or of her life.'

Amber shook her head, not understanding him at all. 'James . . . ?'

He tapped his heels against Cedric's muscular sides and moved off. Looking over his shoulder, he said: 'I can't let you know until we're alone.'

Amber looked about, marvelling that she was gazing upon thousands of years of history. A large step-pyramid loomed up before her, its surfaces worn with time and weather.

'Once, these were covered with smooth stone.'

Turning, Amber saw her father drawing up his camel beside her, his face aglow.

'And do you see the fluted columns at the doorway? Now, come and see here.' He led her to one of the many rectangular buildings, its sides gently inclining. Amber was suddenly gripped with excitement. All her life she had waited while her father went away for months at a time. She had listened to his tales when he returned, fascinated by the stories he told her of beautiful and ornate finds. Now here she was at the entrance to an ancient *mastaba*, its walls richly decorated. Even after so long, she could still make out the faint colour used to paint the graceful scenes.

'Look, here's a scene depicting a scribe,' her father said. 'You can even see the quills laid out ready. These bas-reliefs are fascinating in their detail. All the richness and minutiae of ancient Egyptian life are illustrated there.'

They both dismounted, leaving the

camels in the care of a young boy who whispered softly and patted the creatures as if they were beloved pets.

Davis led his daughter into the structure, down through a narrow corridor. The shadows were thick in places, and Davis had brought a lamp. The dancing flames threw eerie light on carvings of dancers, servants, and women with tall baskets balanced on their heads.

'See here, Amber.' The professor stopped and held up the torch. Hieroglyphic writing was thrown into sharp relief as the light hit the pale yellow carvings. 'This talks of Ankhra, his daily life and his service to the temple. But it doesn't mention Amratep at all. It talks of her father, Hotep.'

Davis pushed his spectacles up his long nose and translated: ''And Hotep was thankful to Ankhra for his devotion to Bast and Horus, who blessed the land with great wealth at harvest.' There — that at least shows that what we know about the priest is true, although there's nothing regarding his thievery here.'

Amber remembered the little book of hieroglyphics she had placed in her handbag. She fished inside and produced it. 'Father, I've brought this. I'd like to look at these carvings for a while, if I may. I'd love to try and decipher some.'

Davis smiled proudly at his daughter. 'I haven't actually worked on this side of the wall yet. I suppose there's no harm in you trying your hand at it.'

Amber grinned. 'You trust me?'

Davis laughed. 'Of course. I shall go down into the next chamber to look at the carvings. Just call me if you need anything.'

She chose a line of hieroglyphics and frowned at it. Well, she would do her best to help her father solve the mystery of the princess and her priest. She chose a distinctive symbol and flicked through her book trying to find it. But after a minute or so of searching, she realised that this was not the way forward.

She puzzled over her problem, trying to recall anything that might help. Then, as she looked at the neat rows of ancient writing, she remembered her father telling her about the Rosetta Stone and Champollion's long quest to decipher the Egyptian writing. She was struck by the fact that he had begun by looking at outlined cartouches that gave names.

She began to look for neatly ringed sets of symbols, and it was not long before she found one. Excited, she set about with a stubby, well-worn pencil and the blank page at the back of the book to work out what name had been inscribed in the stone wall.

Amber was halfway through deciphering the ancient symbols when she was aware of a shadow falling over the carvings. It was the shadow of a man, looming large and rather menacingly. She started and swung round.

'Sorry to disturb you, miss.'

The man who stood before her was very well-spoken and certainly very English. Even in the sweltering heat of Sakkarah, he wore, of all things, a suit of metal-grey. He was tall and thin, his hair receding to show a high forehead glistening with sweat.

'Can I help you?' Amber stepped back, her heart pounding. She could sense that something was wrong. What on earth was a suited man doing in Egypt? He was as out of place as a polar bear here.

'I'm looking for Professor Davis,' explained the man.

Amber stared at him. 'Professor Davis?'

'Yes, my name is — '

'Can I help you? I'm Davis.' The professor came through from the small chamber in which he had been working. His glasses were slipping down his nose and he had a pad of paper in one hand, a pencil in the other.

The man nodded. 'My name is Stamford Baxter. I'm from Baxter,

Baxter & West, solicitors of Oxford Street, London.'

Her father's face took on an incredulous expression. 'Oxford Street? I do trust you haven't followed me all the way to the desert. I know no one who deals with your firm. My own firm is Cash & Chapman.'

'I've been working in Cairo for Mr Hayes. He has his business dealings with us — his new hotel in Luxor.'

Davis frowned. 'Yes. I've been asked by Mr Hayes to look into the archaeology of the site.'

'We'd be most interested in what you have to say about it. I've taken a few weeks to travel down to see the site and will no doubt meet you there. You understand that the go-ahead for the hotel building depends on your findings. That's why we're most keen to be involved in your work. We will be watching with eagle eyes, Professor Davis.'

'Father . . . ' Amber felt that she had to speak. This Stamford Baxter was a most odd man, and her instincts were buzzing like angry bees.

'Ah,' Baxter said. 'Your daughter? How charming. Very pleased to meet you. You must be Amber.'

'You've done some research on me,' the professor said, easing his way slightly in front of Amber. 'I'm grateful for your interest in my progress, and will of course keep you informed. I do not wish to be rude, but I have work to get on with. Good day, Mr Baxter.'

Baxter furnished them both with a polite bow and said his farewell.

Amber clutched at her father's arm. 'I really didn't like him at all,' she said.

Davis hugged his daughter. 'Neither did I, Amber dear. Neither did I.'

Amber had been so shaken by the encounter with the odd solicitor that she and her father had left the *mastaba* and taken a walk through the necropolis. Neither of them could understand fully why Baxter had followed them to Sakkarah, but both were in agreement that something was not right. As they listlessly looked at the step pyramid once more, James and his father joined them.

'Ah, there you are, Davis. It's getting a little cooler now, is it not?' Lachlan Hayes was looking not at Davis, but at Amber. After the worry of Stamford Baxter, it unnerved her greatly that Hayes had not lost his habit of allowing his gaze to wander where a gentleman's should not.

James then gave her an impish look. 'Miss Davis, I hope you've enjoyed looking around here. I hope you're not bored.'

This reminded Amber of her work in the *mastaba*. 'Oh, no, Mr Hayes. I wasn't bored at all. In fact, I was working on some interesting hiero-glyphics. Father, may I give these to you to look at? I'm afraid it's only a little, but it may be of interest.'

The professor took the pad and pocketed it. 'When we return to the boat, I'll be only too glad to look at your findings.'

'Ah, no, Professor. That's what I wanted to speak to you about.' Hayes cleared his throat. 'I'm afraid we won't be able to return to the boat tonight. Apparently there's a problem with the mechanics.'

'But we have our luggage on the boat,' said Amber in despair. 'And where will we sleep?'

'I have a hotel a few miles south of here. It will mean another camel ride, but I'm sure you'll manage. As for luggage, don't worry. The hotel will provide toiletries, and you'll be back on the boat tomorrow.'

'Can we not spend the night on the boat while they work on solving the problem?'

'Ah, I'm afraid not.' Lachlan looked uneasy. 'It is, I'm told, going to be noisy and dusty. I'm also quite sure that the ladies don't wish to be disturbed by the sailors to-ing and fro-ing all night. Most disconcerting and unnecessary. No, I'll pay for your party to stay in the Grand Plaza. It's one of my newest hotels.'

5

The Grand Plaza was certainly the most luxurious hotel that Amber had ever seen. It gleamed with desert colours: deep yellows and golds, with accessories of purest white. The glare of the lamps was tossed back into the marble lobby by mirrors, making the whole place alive with light.

A porter dressed in scarlet with gold frogging came up to the weary party and led them to their respective rooms. Amber and Laura had interconnected rooms next to her father's, Lachlan had an executive suite of heavily gilded rooms on a floor below, and James had a room near to his father's. They said their goodbyes and agreed to meet up for a late supper.

Amber had been given some soap and rose water to wash in, and luckily she had a small bottle of scent in her handbag: a fresh Lily of the Valley fragrance. She freshened up as best she could, and Laura primped at her dress and hair. She still felt uncomfortable in the dress she had worn all day in the searing heat, but there was nothing she could do about it.

James and Lachlan Hayes were already in the dining room, glasses filled and talking in earnest. Amber was struck by the fact that her father was not there, and unaccountably this sent a shiver down her spine.

'Ah, Miss Davis and Miss Dobson.' Lachlan stood up and pulled out two chairs for the ladies to sit. 'I hope you've found your room satisfactory.'

Amber looked around uneasily. Where was her father?

Laura touched her arm softly. 'Mr Hayes asked us if we found our room satisfactory. I should say that we most certainly did, Mr Hayes, thank you.'

Distracted, Amber murmured that the room was fine.

'Are you unwell, Miss Davis?' Lachlan

asked. 'A camel ride and the heat can be upsetting for a delicate young lady.'

Amber could not help snapping: 'I am not delicate. Far from it.'

Laura gave a hiss of surprise at her mistress's show of temper in front of her hosts.

James leant forwards towards Amber. 'You do seem a little under par,' he said. 'Perhaps I could order something for you. A tonic or salts?'

'Do you know where my father is, Mr Hayes?' she asked him, unable to keep the concern out of her voice.

'I believe he's still in his room,' Lachlan answered for his son. 'Are you worried about him, Miss Davis? I have the impression that such a seasoned traveller as your father would have no problems here. He must be used to the heat and dust. It is you who concerns me, as you're unaccustomed to the climate in Egypt.'

'Perhaps you should take your supper in your room, where you'll be more comfortable,' James suggested.

Amber had to agree that she was beginning to feel a headache coming on. Maybe it was the arid air, but she was also sure that something was wrong. Her father, too, had been concerned by the appearance of Stamford Baxter. And, if she were honest, the thought of sitting with Lachlan Hayes and his leering eyes and noisy eating was not pleasant.

The only problem with going to her room was that she would not be with James. His cryptic silliness earlier had tantalised her, and she would have loved to sit and talk with him some more. But it seemed that lying on the chaise longue in her room with the window open might clear her headache.

She excused herself, and Laura came to help her change out of her restrictive stays. She was unlikely to be disturbed, so she would be able to stay in her chemise.

As they passed through the marble reception area, Amber saw a glass-fronted bookcase. She adored reading, and asked the receptionist if she might choose one of the books. He opened the door, and she spent a few happy moments choosing from volumes richly bound in Moroccan leather. She had selected a book on the history of ancient Egypt when she saw, with a quickening of her heart, that Amratep was listed in the index.

Amber had just one more thing to do: she had to check that her father was well. She tapped on his door, and was relieved to hear him say: 'Come in.' Peering round the door, she saw him at a small marble-topped table, studying her notes on the hieroglyphs in the *mastaba*.

'Ah, Amber. I've been looking at the work you did and am very impressed. I shall make an Egyptologist of you yet.'

Amber felt herself glow with pride at his praise. 'Father, supper is ready. But I'm afraid I'm going to my room; I have a headache and I'm tired. I shall have my supper up here, and read.'

Davis peered over his spectacles in

concern. 'You're feeling unwell?'

'Only a mild headache,' Amber reassured him. 'Please don't worry; I'm just hot and weary.'

'Then I shall go down to eat; but if you need anything, you mustn't hesitate to tell me.' He rose from his table and kissed her forehead affectionately. 'Goodnight, my dear.' He then smiled at Laura and said goodnight to her as well. Amber was surprised to see her maid blush at her father's words, and it set her wondering why.

Laura lowered her head, but peeped up at the professor through long, dark lashes. 'Goodnight, sir,' she said in a half-whisper.

Amber took the book to her room and Laura helped her to undress. Once the corset, small bustle and dress were put away, Laura went to ask that super be brought up to her mistress. Amber lay on the chaise longue and opened her book.

A very gentle breeze fluttered in through the window. She gazed down into the garden. It was beautifully arranged in little walled areas of native plants. The scent of jasmine floated up on the air; and she could hear, of all things, a goat in the distance. Dusk was falling, and the stone of the walls was turning a soft rosy hue. Amber let her book fall unread onto her lap.

It was not long before the door clicked open, and a pretty girl brought in a supper of falafel, fish, and various fresh salads. Amber had always wanted to taste the Egyptian food her father talked so enthusiastically about.

* * *

Laura used a bell-pull to ring for someone to come and clear the dishes.

'You look exhausted, Laura,' Amber said. 'Perhaps the day has been too arduous.'

Laura gave a small smile. 'I'm sure I shall get used to being here. I was talking earlier with your father, before he went to take you to the *mastaba*. He told me all sorts of things that I never knew. This country has such a fascinating history. I'm quite sure I'll grow to love being here, despite the risk of heatstroke and freckles.'

Amber laughed. 'So you spoke with my father?'

Laura blushed prettily. 'Well, he . . . we . . . Your father was explaining, as I said, some very interesting facts. I've always been in awe of him; he is so intelligent and . . . ' Here she faltered, her cheeks reddening even more.

'Handsome?' Amber teased.

Laura pursed her lips and stood up quickly. She moved to the opposite window and turned away to look out of it. 'Of course he's handsome, but it's far from me to say such a thing. I'm only an employee.'

'Balderdash!' exclaimed Amber hotly. 'You're not *just* anything. You are Laura, and we love you as a member of our family. You're employed by us, yes, but you mean as much to me as he does.'

Laura turned to her mistress, and Amber could see little drops of moisture in her eyes. 'Really, Miss Amber?'

'Oh, you know you do.' Amber came over and hugged her warmly. 'And I'm glad you think as highly of my father as I do.' Secretly, though, Amber greatly suspected that Laura felt more than admiration for her loving father. Laura, Amber decided, was in love with the professor!

Amber did not say anything about her suspicions. She did not want to embarrass her maid. Instead, she let Laura leave to rest in her room. Amber was tired and achy from her camel ride. She tried to sit and read by the cool air coming through the window, but she couldn't help but go back to thinking about James. She had to admit she had missed his company that evening.

Amber soon drifted off to sleep, the breeze now a colder wind that puffed at her loose, lustrous hair and tugged at the hem of her shift.

She woke up with a start. At first she assumed that the cold had woken her, for now the garden was in darkness, the walls and paths silver in the moonlight. She shivered and rose to close the window. Just as she clicked it shut she stopped, frozen by the sight of two figures slinking along the path towards the back door of the hotel. She could make out only their silhouettes. They were an odd, mismatched pair: one was tall and thin, the other rather bulky with the build of a bulldog. The manner in which they were moving, edging along the foliage and stopping every now and then as if to listen out for something, made her sure they were up to no good.

She pulled on her shawl and tiptoed to the door of Laura's room. Peeping in, she was glad to see her maid fast asleep.

Amber's bare feet padded on the plush gold carpet of the hallway. The corridor walls were adorned with crystal lamps holding tall candles, so it was easy to see which way to go. She followed the corridor past her father's room and down the stairs, which wound down in a spiral. Just as she rounded one twist, she saw a figure coming up towards her.

Her heart lurched and she clutched at the highly polished wood of the banister, chiding herself for being so foolish as to come out by herself.

'Amber?'

It was James! She sighed with relief and ran down the stairs to meet him. Quickly, she explained that she was investigating the two odd men.

'On your own?' He frowned. 'That isn't a good idea.'

Her chin pushed forward defiantly. 'I'm quite capable of being on my own.'

'Yes, but looking for two strange characters at gone midnight, and in your . . . underclothes?'

Amber blushed furiously at the mention of what she was wearing. She had quite forgotten! And now she was with James Hayes. The reddening on her cheeks seemed to make James smile.

'Here, have my jacket,' he said. 'I'd just gone out for a stroll. I've been trying to write my novel, but I just can't seem to get this next chapter right.' He stopped then, and his brows pulled together. 'Are you sure it wasn't me who you saw?'

'I saw two men, definitely, and I'm quite sure they were together. They were acting very oddly, slinking along as if trying to keep out of the light of the windows.'

'And you say they were in the gardens at the back?' He put his jacket around her slender shoulders. Amber shivered at his soft touch.

'My room looks out over the walled gardens, yes, and the back path. It was that path on which they were walking.'

'Then it wasn't me. I was at the front.' James thought for a moment. 'Amber, you go back; I will look for these men. It's possible that they were hotel workers and have a perfectly reasonable explanation for their behaviour, but just in case . . . '

'I want to come with you,' Amber said, prepared to be as stubborn as she needed to be.

James shook his blond head. 'You can't go gallivanting around like that. Besides, if it's dangerous, I'd never forgive myself if anything happened to you.'

Amber found herself looking up into his face, her large brown eyes meeting his dusky gaze. Her breath caught in her throat as he cupped her chin in strong but gentle fingers.

'Isn't it odd that I didn't need to engineer this meeting, as I said I would?' he murmured.

They were interrupted by the sound of glass shattering faintly, as if cushioned by something. James leapt back and put his finger to his lips. Amber found herself grasping at his sleeve. They made their way down the rest of the stairs, and James led her towards the back of the hotel, through the empty lobby which was softly lit by the moon and a few well-cleaned oil lamps.

They were about to enter a dark corridor that led to the back entrance when they heard a scuffle and urgent, hushed voices. James indicated with a wave of his hand for Amber to stay back. He moved slowly into the passageway and was swallowed up by the gloom. The sound of her blood rushing in her ears was all Amber could hear. She realised that she was shaking with apprehension.

Suddenly there was a cacophony of yells and shouts. Amber gave a squeal of alarm; and then, without thinking about it, rushed into the passage to help James.

She ran headlong into someone and began to pummel at the taut body with small fists. She was grabbed around the waist and hoisted up over a shoulder.

She screamed and tried to wriggle free of the grasp, but the barbarian who held her had her in a tighter grip than she could cope with, and she knew she was helpless. She yelled for James as she was carried off. Then she began to spit a few choice words, telling her kidnapper just what she thought of him. But then it struck her that she was being taken back into the hotel; and when her abductor reached the lobby with its pale circles of yellow light, she was mortified to find that it was James who held her.

'You are a little wildcat!' He put her down gently and pushed long fingers through her tousled hair. 'I hope Laura never sees or hears you in such a frightful temper. My ears are quite burnt.'

Amber bit her lip in embarrassment. 'Was it you I hit?'

James rubbed a hand over his stomach. 'You pack quite a punch there, Amber m'dear.'

'I thought it was one of the men who . . . ' Her voice trailed off. Her mortification was complete.

'But I'm flattered that you were so brave as to come and try to rescue me.

I had to carry you off so unceremoniously because I was afraid the two housebreakers would return and you'd have three men to fight off. I feared for their safety.'

'You mean they escaped?'

'We scared them off. We shall tell my father about this, and he can inform the authorities. I'm sure they were only bungling burglars. They must have assumed, quite rightly, that there were rich pickings in a place such as this. Well done, Amber. It is because of you that nothing awful happened.'

Amber had a feeling that the men had not just been simply robbers. Her instincts were fired up now. Something was not right. She was about to explain her fears to James when a light suddenly blazed; then another, and another. Lamps were being turned up; and when she looked up the stairwell she saw her father, Laura and Lachlan Hayes rushing down towards the marble lobby.

Her father reached her first. 'Amber!

What's happening?' He looked from James to his daughter, and back to James. 'Amber?'

Lachlan Hayes brooked no such soft approach and marched straight up to his son with thunder in his face. 'There had better be a good explanation for this, James,' he blustered. 'Well, is there? I can only imagine why you insist on causing Miss Davis to be compromised and embarrassed.'

'There were two men breaking in,' James explained. 'Amber came down to see, and I was here after a late walk. I had writer's block.'

'Writers' block? Men breaking in? Do you expect me to believe that a sensible young lady like Miss Davis would come down here, so attired, to apprehend burglars? You are a disappointment to me, James. I shall not allow any more. Now go, and leave us. I expect you to be gone tomorrow morning. You will go back to Cairo, and when I return I'll make arrangements for you to go and take over the running of the European hotels. I think a few years of travelling to Paris, Rome and London will cool this foolishness.'

'But Mr Hayes — ' Amber tried to put in her version of events, but was stopped by a wave of Lachlan's hand.

'Miss Davis, you mustn't allow my son to upset you. He'll be gone tomorrow and you need not be worried by his boorishness any longer. Perhaps your maid can help you back to your room.'

Laura threw a murderous look at James and put protective arms around her charge. 'I'm sure that Miss Amber will welcome a rest,' she said pointedly.

As Laura and Amber moved off, Amber could hear Hayes tell his son: 'If I see you tomorrow, I will not be responsible for my actions. You will leave, and I hope never to set eyes on such a wastrel as you again.'

Amber felt hot, angry tears prick her eyes. She could not believe that Lachlan would speak like that to his son. Why had he not listened to their explanation? If he had only listened, he would have surely been filled with gratitude to know that they had stopped the hotel from being ransacked. But then, as she climbed wearily into her bed, she wondered once again if that had been the reason for the break-in.

First the odd Stamford Baxter, and now these two men. It seemed strange that such things were suddenly happening around her. However, her most immediate concern was the painful twisting knot in her stomach caused by the imminent and forced departure of James. She could not imagine her trip through Egypt without him, and the manner in which he now had to leave made it worse.

She would never see him again. With this dismal thought she fell asleep, tears staining her cheeks.

6

At breakfast the next day, Lachlan Hayes informed his guests that his son had left the Grand Plaza in disgrace and was expected to return to the capital. 'He will wait there until I have returned,' Hayes said, peering at Amber with piggish eyes. 'I'm sure you're glad he has gone, Miss Davis. He's sorely tried you, I think.'

'There really was an attempted break-in last night,' Amber insisted, her heart raw at losing James.

'You don't have to keep up this pretence for him,' Hayes said. 'I know what a sensible girl you are, and I'm quite sure you would never dream of leaving your room dressed only in . . . unmentionable garments.' Here he moistened his plump lips with his tongue, and a horrid flush spread across his cheeks. He mopped at his brow.

Amber bristled. 'It was no pretence, sir. I assure you that there — '

Davis held up his hand and spoke quietly to his daughter. 'Amber, you're obviously tired after your adventure last night. Why don't you finish breakfast, then rest a while until we can go back to the *Amethyst Sea*?'

Amber felt that she could do nothing else. As she made her way once more up the wide, winding staircase, she decided to peep into James's room. She knocked first, and upon receiving no answer, she looked in. It was sparse and obviously unoccupied. James had definitely gone.

The party returned to the *Amethyst Sea*. Amber and Laura immediately asked that hot water be provided for bathing, and Hayes told them to come to the lounge for drinks and snacks after the excitement of the previous day.

Amber chose a peacock-blue satin that shimmered and gave the illusion of changing colours as she moved. Laura stood back and gave a sigh of satisfaction. 'You look lovely, miss.'

A thought struck Amber. It was a mischievous thought, but one that appealed greatly the more she thought about it. 'Laura, why don't you borrow one of my dresses? I'm sure you can find one to fit.'

Laura looked aghast. 'Miss, I couldn't! I'm quite happy in my own clothes. The very idea! What would your father think?'

Amber smiled to herself. That had been just what she had wondered. 'I order you to try one on,' she laughed. 'I think my pink one will suit. It will go with your colouring.'

Laura flinched. 'I couldn't.'

'Nonsense.' Amber rummaged in her jewellery box. 'This dress calls for pearls.'

'Are you suggesting I wear your jewels too?' Laura took a step back. 'That would surely be going too far.'

'Laura, dear, let me see how well this pearl pendant suits. See, it's only a very simple teardrop, but it will sit nicely with the pink. Do try it on, for me. Let me have my whims.'

Amber helped Laura get into the dress. The cut defined her maid's figure and set off the gentle roses in her cheeks. Amber then had a few happy minutes of dressing Laura's pale blonde hair into curls that she then pulled into a soft knot at the nape of her neck. She let small twists and ringlets fall around her maid's pretty face.

'Now see,' Amber said, turning Laura to the mirror. 'Exquisite.'

And indeed she did look lovely. They took one last look in the mirror and went to the lounge. As they walked into the room, Professor Davis looked up from where he had been discussing something with Hayes. His mouth fell open and he stared.

'Well,' said Hayes, 'I'm surely experiencing a mirage.'

'Is that my daughter's dress, Laura?' asked Davis.

Laura swallowed and went pink. 'Yes sir. I'm sorry. I shall change.'

'No!' Davis cleared his throat. 'I mean to say that it suits you well, Laura. It's an admirable colour.'

'Oh.' She seemed at a loss for words.

'Yes, she looks lovely, doesn't she, Father?' Amber grinned.

'Indeed. And so do you, dear.'

'Well, after yesterday we needed to feel fresh as daises and just as lovely!' quipped Amber.

She watched her father. He had a look on his face that could only indicate one thing. As he turned to Laura, their heads seemed to move a little closer. Laura's gentle fingers briefly touched the professor's sleeve. Davis laughed more than Amber had ever known. They were in love. It made Amber ache for James. She wondered what he was doing now. Was he making his way back to Cairo?

★　★　★

The journey was not so exciting now that James wasn't on board. Amber often wondered what he'd meant to tell her when they were alone. He had been about to tell her when they were interrupted by the break-in. She could still feel his strong, warm fingers cupping her chin. She had even convinced herself that he had been about to kiss her.

It was just such thoughts that were occupying her mind one evening when she was alone on the deck. She had been reading the book she'd borrowed from the hotel, after asking Lachlan Hayes if she might borrow it for the duration of her stay. She had let the book fall to her lap as she once more watched the valleys and banks pass by.

She was interrupted by someone coming up behind her. At first she assumed it to be her father or Laura, but when she turned she realised it was Lachlan Hayes.

'Oh, Mr Hayes,' she said, twisting round to get a view of him. 'I'm sorry, I didn't see you there.'

'Daydreaming, eh?' he asked, his

pudgy fingers now closing over the back of Amber's chair.

'As always.' She gave a small, brittle laugh. His proximity intimidated her somewhat, and she suddenly felt very vulnerable.

'Miss Davis, may I sit with you? There are servants about preparing luncheon, so we are not quite alone. But alone enough.'

Amber felt a shiver and shrank back a little from her host. 'Alone enough for what, Mr Hayes?'

'I will, of course, speak with your father, but I wanted to see what you thought first.'

'About what exactly, sir?'

'I would be most interested in your opinion on becoming my wife.'

Amber almost retched in horror. Indeed, her small fingers flew to her mouth. 'Your wife?'

Hayes looked down at his feet. 'I see that it is not something you find appealing,' he said.

'I'm sorry, Mr Hayes, but you

shocked me. And have I understood that you haven't spoken to my father on this matter?'

'A trifle unconventional maybe, but I really was keen to see your reaction to the matter. I am a lot older than you, granted, but I have money.'

'I see,' Amber said quietly.

'If you married me, then I could keep you in very good style.'

Amber sat rigid and tense, as if moving would cause some horrid reaction. Hayes wished her to be his wife! The thought was awful. Then she had an idea. 'Mr Hayes, sir, your offering for me is very kind, but I could not leave my father. We are, as you have seen, very close, and I've always said that I wouldn't leave him alone.'

Hayes gave her a slow smile. 'But my dear, if you were to marry me, we'd live in my house in Hampshire. It is, I assure you, large enough for your father to have his own suite of rooms, quite private. I wouldn't dream of separating the two of you. And of course, I would be happy to provide any money your father needed to continue his research.'

Amber was stunned. She knew that money was one problem that made it difficult for her father to continue his work. He had struggled to save for this trip by lecturing and even taking private pupils who were cramming for exams.

'The house will be emptier now that James will be running around Europe for me,' Hayes said slyly. 'But I'm sure he'd come home for Christmas and such. He seemed quite fond of you; I'm sure he'd be delighted to have you as a stepmother.'

Amber stood up shakily. 'I'm sorry, Mr Hayes, but what you suggest is out of the question.'

'Even if I would look after you and your father? You should have no money concerns at all.'

'There is, I believe, a word for women who will sell anything for money.' She picked up her book. 'I am not such a woman.' With that, she fled to her room, tears burning her throat and eyes.

★ ★ ★

Laura found Amber weeping and immediately took control of the situation. Amber found that she could not keep her worries to herself any longer, so she told her maid about her feelings for James, her concerns that something was simply not right, and how she had been proposed to by Lachlan Hayes. Laura listened, then brought Amber some cool water and some rose-scented lotion. Amber washed and freshened her tear-streaked face.

'I thought there was something about Lachlan Hayes,' Laura said disapprovingly. 'I knew that man was not a nice person. Fancy offering for someone young enough to be his daughter. And as for James . . . well.' She pursed her lips. 'You must accept that he's gone; although from what you say, he was only trying to stop those robbers. But I must say that when I saw you with him . . . I nearly died from the shock.'

Smiling a little through her tears, Amber said, 'I'm sorry, Laura.'

'I suppose you'll feel better once we get to the site. You've always wanted to see your father at work.'

7

Lachlan Hayes seemed to keep his distance, suddenly, from Amber. He only spoke briefly and politely at meals or if they met in passing. Denied James's company, Amber spent most of her time reading or with her father, looking over his work regarding Amratep.

It was when they were only two days away from Karnak that the professor suddenly exclaimed, 'Oh Lord, how could I have forgotten?'

Surprised by his sudden outburst, Amber dropped the pen she had been using to copy up some facts from the book she had borrowed from the hotel. 'What is it? Forgotten what?'

'Your notes from Sakkarah,' Davis said, hunting amongst the mess of notes and books on the little desk. 'I meant to mention it, but what with one thing and another, it just slipped my mind.'

Amber, too, had completely forgotten the notes she had made. Her father found the little notebook under a pile of foolscap and opened it at the back page where she had begun deciphering the picture writing. 'This was from a line containing a cartouche, yes?' he asked.

'Yes, but I didn't quite finish the line. The cartouche was difficult to decipher; but as I worked on it, I just came across the meanings of the other symbols.'

'See here, Amber.' Davis once more rummaged around the untidy desk and produced a cream-coloured piece of correspondence paper. 'This, I think, looks like your cartouche.'

Amber frowned at it and then shrugged her slender shoulders. 'I think so. Yes, I remember this bird-like sign.'

'Then read this.' He wrote something beneath the copy of the cartouche and showed it to his daughter. Amber read 'AMRATEP'.

'The writing I was deciphering was

about Amratep?' Amber was incredulous. The answer to the riddle may have been in their hands. If Baxter had not interrupted and worried them, they might have had the biggest possible lead yet.

'It looks as if it was. Read what you managed to work out.'

Amber took the book. ' 'The sun and stars shall know the devotion of Am — ' '

'Yes, Amratep, I'm sure. It's very lyrical, but I suspect it refers to the princess making offerings to the gods at the temple.'

'Which would tie in with the priest,' Amber said excitedly.

'So we're nearer to establishing that she did exist. But now we need to find out what happened to her. Or could even the writing at Sakkarah be a myth?'

'Is that possible?' Amber poured some lemonade for them and sat back down.

'We need to get to the site in Luxor.'

'Will our stop in Karnak help us, do you think?'

'In Karnak I'm hoping simply to see the temple and show you and Laura. Karnak has been my own speciality, and I have exhausted all possible leads there.' Davis took a long drink of his lemonade. 'Though there's still much of the area unexplored archaeologically, I have no time. It's to be my next project; I hope to come across Hotep's site at least. I'm sure there will be something there. However, for the time being, we shall content ourselves with being tourists. I miss Karnak, my dear . . . I've worked there for nearly ten years, and it's like a second home to me.'

Amber laughed. 'I'm aware of that.'

Her father did not laugh. 'Do you mean to say that I'm rarely in London?'

Amber swallowed. 'I simply meant that I know how much this work means to you.'

'You may be right in thinking that I've been too far from home on too many occasions.'

Amber suddenly felt sorrowful. 'I can't deny that I've missed you terribly, Father. But sharing this experience with you — being here in Egypt — has made me feel closer.' She gave him an impromptu hug. 'And I know Laura appreciates it, too.'

The professor's cheeks coloured. 'Ah, does she? Oh, well, I'm glad she's enjoying the experience.'

'I think she's enjoying the company, to be honest.'

'She sees you every day, and I get the impression that she's not very fond of Mr Lachlan Hayes.'

Amber pulled away slightly from her father's warm arms and smiled down into his face. 'You know whose company I mean.'

'Are you referring to me?'

'Yes. I think Laura is fond of you.'

Davis gently manoeuvred his daughter back into her seat and stood up. 'Amber, do you mean that, or are you jesting?'

'I mean it.'

'I must admit to a certain fondness for her as well, but I imagine it's born of the gratitude I hold for her taking such wonderful care of you.'

'And the fact that she's a lovely, attractive and caring woman.' Amber tapped a pencil on the table rhythmically. 'Oh Father, if you should only ask her to marry you . . . I can't imagine anything better.'

Davis slumped back into his chair. 'Amber, can you not see how difficult that would be? She's an employee, and would feel very uncomfortable if I broached such a subject.'

'I don't imagine she would. She really is fond of you too,' Amber assured him.

'I'll hear no more of this silliness.' Her father was rarely strict with her, but on this occasion it seemed as if his word was law. Amber mentioned the subject no more, but knew that the match would be perfect.

★　★　★

Karnak Temple was two hundred and fifty acres, dedicated to the god Amun. Amber had, of course, read her father's book about the site, but even that had not prepared her for the sheer breath-taking sight of one of the largest temples in the world.

'You can see why this temple was so awe-inspiring,' Davis said as Amber and Laura gazed up at the pillars, which showed gold in the sunlight. 'This temple is so big that one could fit the whole of Notre Dame in it.'

Columns, ram-headed sphinxes and obelisks loomed up, while pillars formed carved forests around them. Amber suddenly felt very humble, insignificant and small.

'I can't imagine what it must have looked like in its full glory,' Laura breathed.

'I've often tried,' admitted the profes-sor, smiling warmly at Laura. 'But I confess that I cannot.'

Amber said: 'I would love to see the Sacred Lake. Where is it?'

Davis pointed southwards. 'You'll need to go past the Hypostyle Hall. The lake is walled, but please be careful. In fact, I shall come with you.'

'No, no. I'm fine,' Amber assured him. 'You do your own business, Father. You might show Laura the Avenue of the Sphinxes. I'd like to be on my own for a while. After all, I've been waiting so long to see this that I feel quite overwhelmed.'

Davis looked dubious, but probably knew better than to argue with his daughter. He looked at the worried Laura and said: 'Very well. Laura, shall we go? I imagine there's much I can show you.'

'But will Miss Amber be all right?'

'She will — won't you, Amber? Ah, look — there's a group of tourists with a guide. We can follow their route. I think they must be heading for the Sanctuary of Montu.' Davis led Laura to the group of tourists, who were fanning themselves whilst listening to their guide.

Amber tied the ribbons of her sunbonnet under her chin and made her way towards the lake. She had to navigate through gigantic structures, winding her way through avenues and courtyards. People meandered around, gaping up tongue-tied at these huge wonders of the ancient world.

About halfway through the unshaded avenue of statutes, she began to feel that someone was watching or even following her. She turned around more than once, but could see no one of note except a veiled woman whom she had seen since turning into the strip. She knew it was the same lady because her clothes were so brightly coloured that she could not possibly be mistaken. The head covering concealed any features; Amber could not make out her face at all.

The veiled woman stopped walking, now making no attempt to hide the fact that she was interested in Amber. Amber looked around her. She had wandered into a courtyard that was shaded by tall walls carved with high hieroglyphics. No one else was around. It was just her and the mysterious woman.

Amber tried to look relaxed, musing over the carvings whilst still very aware of the stranger watching her. The hairs on the back of her neck bristled, and she knew she would have to do something. She turned to say something to the woman and squealed as she did so. The lady had moved swiftly and silently and was now standing only a few steps away from her. Amber stared as the veil was pulled from the face.

'James?' She almost fainted when the dark cloth was peeled back to reveal the handsome features of James Hayes. 'What on earth are you doing here — and dressed like that? I thought you were in Cairo.'

James grinned. 'Yes, and I expect my father does as well. Listen, I couldn't simply leave. I'm not going to be ordered about by my unreasonable father.'

'I tried to explain to him what really happened in the Grand Plaza,' Amber said, 'but he refused to listen.'

James shook his head, which was still covered by a mantle. 'I know. He's quite brutish when he feels that his ideas are being challenged.'

'But where are you staying? What are you doing?'

'I wonder, Amber, if you noticed a small boat that followed you up the Nile?'

She frowned in thought. 'There are quite a few boats on the river, and I can't say that any one has stood out.'

'A white one with apple green letters — *The Wandering Sphynx*.'

She could not remember such a vessel, and told him so.

'It's a friend's boat. He's doing the Grand Tour before taking to the Bar, and has a boat that he's using to take a few friends sightseeing. I jumped on board. And I've disembarked with you now to follow you, dressed like this so as not to attract attention. I can't risk my father seeing me.'

Amber raised an eyebrow. 'I see. So all this time you've been following us.'

'And watching you. I see that you spend a deal of time gazing out over the water, thinking. Tell me, what do you think about?'

'My father seems very much taken with Laura,' she said eventually. 'And she with him. I'm hoping that they both see sense and join together.'

'You're not thinking of your own sweetheart?'

The glow in her cheeks now became a fire. 'What sweetheart? I have no such thing!'

'No beau waiting for you back in London?'

'Certainly not!'

'No sad and mournful lad watching the moon and sighing over you?'

'I think this is a very silly and rather fresh conversation.' She shook herself and tried to act prim. 'Now, if you'll excuse me, I'm making my way to the Sacred Lake. You're welcome to join me if you replace your veil.' She walked away towards the lake.

James ran after her, holding his cumbersome skirts. 'Great Scott, how do women manage such ridiculous clothes?' he panted, catching her up easily despite the hindrance of his female attire. 'Now, Amber, I promised you that I'd tell you something when we were alone.'

Her heart hammered. 'Yes?' She couldn't keep her voice steady.

'I knew from the moment that I set eyes on you that you were an exceptional girl. And, despite my father's sternness and your maid's view that I'm a cad, I think you and I have struck up something of a friendship.'

Amber agreed. 'Is that what you wished to say?'

'No. I'm trying to tell you that . . .' He suddenly pulled the veil back over his face and stooped a little, as if to lessen his height.

'*Naam, naam.*' His voice became thin, and Amber was quite amused that he could suddenly seem to become this Arab woman.

'Miss Davis, is that lady troubling you?' It was Lachlan Hayes.

Amber stiffened. 'No, no. She was just telling me the way to the Sacred Lake. I got lost. She can speak a little English.'

'Well, your maid and your father have been with the tour group, and I've been to see some of the wonders of this place. It would make a great hotel if renovated.'

'Surely you're joking, sir,' Amber said uneasily.

'Miss Davis, money can buy most things.'

'But not thousands of years of rich history, or such wonderful antiquities as these.'

Hayes shrugged his wide shoulders. 'I doubt people think of that now. These are modern times. People want a future, not a dusty past. Now, perhaps this lady will accompany us to the lake.'

James made a solemn bow and

muttered, '*Naam*' — yes.

The three walked out of the shaded courtyard and back into the brilliance of the sun. Eventually, after a few minutes of uncomfortable silence, Hayes turned to Amber.

'We have a chaperone of sorts, but I doubt she'll understand our conversation. I mean to speak to you about my recent proposal. I'd like to urge you to reconsider.'

Next to her, Amber could feel James tense. She kept her head lowered; she could not look at either James or his father. 'I'm sorry, but my mind is unchanged.'

'I would expect very little from you, Miss Davis. I perhaps would expect a son to inherit my wealth after I am gone.'

Amber stood frozen. 'Sir, you have a son.'

'I'm very disheartened by James. He's a waste of space. All this writing and such; he should be wanting to make a life for himself.'

'Am I to understand that you wish to marry me so that you can have a son to disinherit James?' Amber could not bear to look at her disguised companion. What must he be feeling, concealed under his shroud and listening to this defamation of his character by his own father?

'In a way, but it's more than that,' Hayes answered. 'You would make a sweet companion in my twilight years. And you would be a pretty and genial hostess at the many functions I host for brokers, bankers and such.'

'A token wife, then. No more than a bauble and a smile to win you more money.' Amber glared up at him. 'And I would not stoop so low as to be party to a plan to push James out of your life.'

'But it would be your own son who would inherit. Surely you would not be offended at that?'

'Yes, Mr Hayes, I'm afraid I would,' Amber said, icily calm.

'Ah well, then. I suppose your father

will continue to struggle for money, and maybe you'll end up a spinster. There are very few men who would take on the professor as well as you. And I know of no one who would finance his work.'

Amber began to walk on ahead. She glanced at James as she passed, but of course the disguise obscured his features. She was glad she couldn't see the look on his face.

Hayes caught up with her and took her elbow. 'Amber, I urge you to think about this. It would be in everyone's best interests. I'm confident you can see that. In fact . . . ' He reached into the inside breast pocket of his jacket and pulled out a little velvet pouch, which he handed to her.

She looked at it, feeling the plush fabric and realising there was a small, hard object inside. She opened it and took out a ring: a smooth piece of blue lapis lazuli encased in a gold claw that stood proudly on the small gold band. Amber looked at it, feeling numb, aware only of James's proximity. How hurt he must be feeling to hear his own father talk so cruelly about him.

'Amber, I want you to have this ring,' Lachlan was saying. 'I promise I'll put my proposal to your father. Maybe he'll see the perfect sense it makes.'

'No, Mr Hayes. I . . . there's someone else, sir. I couldn't lie to you.' She ran off, her skirts swishing around her ankles.

* * *

The Sacred Lake was as still as a looking-glass, splinters of brilliant light reflecting from the sun. Amber stood in the shade of a large fringed tree, gazing out over the water. Neither Lachlan nor James had followed her. It had taken her a while to locate and reach the lake. Why had she told Hayes that there was someone else?

In her mind she had been thinking, of course, of James. She was beginning to wonder if she should simply tell

James the truth — which was that she was very, very fond of him, but that the idea of leaving her father alone was too painful. Her mind was a whirl of emotion.

She slid down to sit on the dusty, sandy floor. Her skirts would get dirty and Laura would bemoan the fact, but she was too tired and the heat was intense. The shade of the tree barely sheltered her. She pulled the sunhat a little over her face and found that her eyes were heavy. She must have fallen asleep, because she was suddenly jolted awake by a voice.

'Miss Davis? Are you all right?'

She shot to her feet and gasped. Before her stood Stamford Baxter!

'You mustn't fall asleep in this heat, Miss Davis, even in the shade of a tree. Perhaps you're lost? I shall help you find your father and maid.'

Amber rearranged her crumpled and creased clothes. 'No, Mr Baxter, I am perfectly well, thank you. I know where they are. I'm probably late.' She looked at the little silver watch pinned, brooch-like, to the front of her dress. She had not made any arrangements to meet again with her father and Laura, but she would tell Baxter she had, so that he thought she would be expected. 'Goodness, they will be wondering where I have got to.' She made to hurry off, but Baxter took her elbow in a firm grip.

'I would be happier if you let me accompany you, Miss Davis. It's still hot, and I fear you may feel a little dazed by the heat.'

His manner set alarms jangling in Amber's head. There was no way she would allow him to walk with her. She shook her arm free. 'Thank you, sir, but I'm perfectly all right.'

Baxter's demeanour changed. His eyes narrowed, and his thin, tall frame loomed over her. 'I really don't want to argue, Miss Davis. But I think that your father will be most upset that I let you wander around alone.'

'My father will feel no such thing,'

Amber said curtly. 'I must be going, Mr Baxter.' She hurried off.

'Miss Davis, come back. I insist.'

Amber began to stride, her one thought being to get away. Baxter was suddenly close behind. Now she knew that she was in danger. She picked up her skirts and fled back down the statue-lined avenue that had led her to the lake. She found herself in a maze of similar paths.

Baxter was close on her heels. She could hear his panting, struggling breath. Trying to put distance between herself and her pursuer, she ran past pillars and obelisks, slipping between them. It then occurred to her to climb onto one of the small platforms on which the pillars were mounted.

She watched Baxter search through the rows of posts. He came closer to the section in which she was hiding, and her insides quivered. Then he was out of view, and she could not work out in which direction he had gone. She tried to hold her breath steady, clinging to the stone and wondering if he could hear her heart beating, as it seemed to boom out of her, filling this quiet part of the temple.

Amber closed her eyes briefly, willing herself not to panic. She was almost faint with the fear and the heat. She opened her eyes to see the rainbow hues of a woollen skirt pass by. James in his disguise!

'James!' she hissed. 'James!'

The figure stopped and stood as if listening. The veil was slowly pulled from the head. James frowned up. Amber kicked a small rock onto the sandy floor by his feet. He started and peered up, shielding his grey eyes. 'Amber?'

'Shh — just wait for me.' She scrambled down, leaping the last little bit to land in his waiting arms.

'Oh James, I'm being followed! Do you remember me telling you about Stamford Baxter? I was right — he isn't all he seems. He's been chasing me. Please help me find my father and

Laura, and then we can get back to the boat.'

'Surely we must find this pursuer? I dread to think what might have happened to you if he'd got hold of you.'

'I know.' Her voice had a tremble, and she felt very weak. It was only then that it occurred to her that she was still in James's arms. She looked into his eyes and saw an unreadable expression. 'James, your father said some wicked things today. I don't . . . '

He shook his head. 'Don't.' He placed her back on the ground. 'He gave you a ring. He wants to marry you.'

'But I won't marry him,' she said earnestly.

'I know you won't. I heard you telling him there was someone else. But tell me, Amber, why did you deny it when I asked that very question?'

'James, I want you to listen. I only meant . . . ' It suddenly seemed as if James was far away, his image darkening and fading. He spoke to her, but the voice drifted over her as if not connected to anything. She thought how odd it was that the temple ruins were swaying after all these years of standing. Then blackness enveloped her.

8

Voices drifted towards her, but she really did not want to wake. She was tired, and the sandy ground was soft and warm. Then gentle arms lifted her, and she was nestled against a familiar chest. Familiar cologne and the soft voice of her father gave her the impetus to try and come round. Her dark eyes opened, and her father's dear face was looking down at her.

'She must have got too hot,' Laura said, kneeling by Amber and fanning her.

'I shouldn't have let her leave on her own.' Davis stroked back his daughter's glossy hair. 'I'm sorry, Amber. It's a good job this kind woman helped you.'

Amber groggily looked up at James. 'Y . . . yes.'

Davis began to speak to James in Arabic. James nodded and murmured.

The professor handed him some coins. Then Amber held her breath as James once again unveiled himself. Laura gave a squeak and Davis gasped.

'I can explain this.' James began to peel away the robe to reveal his usual attire. 'I couldn't leave. I tailed the *Amethyst Sea* in a friend's boat. Dressing like this has been the only way to follow you. Now that you know I'm still around, I'd better go and explain to my father.' He sighed. 'I can't expect any of you to keep this from him.'

'It seems a little odd that my daughter has been in your company alone on two occasions,' Davis said.

'Father,' Amber pleaded, 'please don't.'

'And on both occasions it seems that she's been in some danger.' He turned to Amber, who was struggling to sit up.

James held out his hand. 'I need to explain something, Professor.' He proceeded to tell Amber's father all about the attempted break-in at the hotel, and explained that Baxter was chasing her.

'It is all true,' Amber said when he had finished.

'Well, Mr Hayes, I am indebted to you. I'm grateful that you always seem to be there when Amber needs help.' Davis helped his shaky daughter to her feet. 'Both Amber and I knew that Stamford Baxter was odd. It seems he was a miscreant after all. I'm only glad that Amber was able to get away. So, Mr Hayes, if you wish us to keep your secret, I for one am willing to do so.'

Amber hugged him. 'Thank you, Father. I'm sure James will appreciate that.'

'If you'll excuse me, Professor Davis,' James said, 'I think I ought to tell my father. I've decided to go to Cairo after all and await his return. I'll go to Europe. I had thought that there was something for me here, but I believe I was wrong.'

Amber's fingers fluttered to her mouth. 'Leave? No, you can't.'

'I must. It's the only way.'

'Mr Hayes,' put in Davis, 'may I

suggest that you accompany us back to the boat? I'll explain my gratitude to your father; you can finish the trip with us and then make your way back when we all leave for Cairo. I know your father was angry with you; but if I explain the circumstances, I can only imagine that he'll be willing to reconsider.'

James's eyes were unaccountably cold. 'But as I said, I have nothing here. My writing is stale, my book lies unfinished in a drawer, and I have to think of my future.' When he lifted his eyes and met Amber's own large brown ones, the look he gave chilled her. 'I would hate my father to feel that he has to disown me.'

Davis put a friendly hand on his arm. 'My dear sir, I really don't think your father will feel that to be necessary.'

'I think you should speak to him about it. I thank you for your gracious offer to talk to him, Professor, but I'll speak to him myself.' He turned to go.

'Wait!' Laura rushed up to him. 'Mr

Hayes, I admit to being very wary of Miss Amber enjoying your company. However, now that the situation has been explained to me, I'm so glad that you've been there on the occasions when she needed you. Please, Mr Hayes, let Professor Davis speak to your father. It's the least we can do.'

James looked at Amber and sighed. 'Very well, Miss Dobson. I'd be thankful for any bridges that could be mended between my father and me.'

Laura smiled warmly. 'Then let's go back to the boat. Poor Miss Amber looks quite done in.'

★   ★   ★

'Professor Davis, I can only imagine that you're simply being kind to my son,' said Lachlan Hayes. 'I couldn't possibly allow you to labour under the misapprehension that he's some sort of hero.' He took a large swig of brandy. 'Miss Davis, I think it's about time that I discussed with your father our little understanding.'

Amber was sitting on the sofa in the lounge of the *Amethyst Sea*, having bathed and changed. Lachlan came to her and gently took her small hand. Amber saw her father swallow and his cheeks pale. She felt giddy again and sick, knowing that her face must also be blanched.

'I've asked your daughter to marry me, sir,' Hayes said. 'I know that I should have discussed the matter with you first, of course, but I wanted to gauge her initial reaction.'

Davis slowly and deliberately put down his glass and said: 'And what was her reaction?'

Hayes gave a polite cough, a little clearing of the throat. 'She's rather timid and modest. I understand that she wishes time to consider and was also concerned that I talk to you about it.'

'Amber?' Davis's face was puckered at the brow and his lips formed a tight line. 'What say you to this?'

Amber had to lie back on her cushions. 'I'm afraid I had to decline, and I told Mr Hayes so. Perhaps he misunderstood.' The plush room began to spin.

'Then there's your answer, Mr Hayes.' Davis strode over to the sofa and sat beside Amber. 'Now, she's unwell. I'd like her maid to come and help her to her room. Today's excitement has quite worn her out.'

Hayes sighed. 'Then that's that.' He dropped Amber's hand. 'I'm sorry you feel that way, Miss Davis. But it's your choice. If you'll excuse me, I need to speak with my son. That's another problem for me.' He fairly stormed from the room.

Amber clung to her father's hand. 'Father, I hope you don't think ill of me? He told me that you'd live in the house too, and that he'd give you money for your work. If you want that, then I'll marry him.'

Davis looked shocked. 'Amber! How could you imagine that I'd let you do such a thing? I don't want my precious daughter to marry simply for money. I would never want that.'

Laura came in and helped Amber back to her room. As she lay in bed, she remembered the tiny velvet bag with the ring in it. She had placed it in her handbag. She retrieved it from the bedside table and took out the ring. It was beautiful; the blue of the stone pure and lustrous. But of course, Lachlan Hayes did not love her, and this ring was not a token of love; it was simply a symbol of his wealth.

She replaced the ring and put the bag back on the bedside table. At least her father was not upset that she had refused Hayes. To be honest, she had never expected him to be.

She pulled the blanket over herself and closed her eyes.

* * *

Amber fanned herself and was glad of her wide-brimmed sunbonnet. The

119

party had docked in Luxor and had hired three brightly painted carriages to take them to the camp. Laura and Amber sat in one, the professor and Hayes in another, while James and the bags took the last. Amber's own small open-topped carriage was pulled by a horse the colour and sheen of a chestnut, and he tossed a proud head as he moved through the streets.

They passed the lively bazaar, and Amber and Laura peered in amazement at the stalls of bright garments, the baskets of fruit, and the men with their musical pipes. Then they wound their way through Luxor's narrow streets, which were filled with stalls bearing strangely scented spices and jewellery.

The heat and the dryness intensified as they rode on, and eventually they reached the edge of the archaeologists' camp. Large tents had been erected, and workmen were carefully clearing the area while others carried trays of pottery shards to an awning under which were long tables.

Amber allowed James to help her and Laura out of the carriage. She watched her father march purposefully towards the awning, and then she followed. On the table were eroded ancient tools and weapons.

'Ah, Professor Davis.' An Egyptian, whose wide smile immediately endeared him to Amber, greeted them.

'Saidi!' Davis seemed delighted to see the man. 'Amber, this is Hammed Saidi. He was a student of mine when I lectured at Oxford.'

Hammed shook hands with her. 'I am Anglo-Egyptian,' he explained. 'I stayed with my mother's family in England while studying. It was your father who inspired me.'

Amber was delighted that Hammed Saidi was so kind about her father. He began to discuss the excavation thus far with Davis. Amber listened, fascinated, as he talked of shabti funerary figures and scarab beetles. 'And now I'm sure you're anxious to see the tomb,' he said.

Amber could not hold back her

eagerness. They had travelled four hundred and fifty miles up the Nile to see this. And she had waited a lifetime.

The mud-brick tomb was entered via a small, craggy hand-cut shaft. The professor and Amber descended a few steps. The walls were black, with only faint light coming from glowing torches attached by workers to the sides of the tomb.

Amber followed her father, keeping her hand to the dry wall so as not to stumble. As Hammed had warned, they were met by a narrow passage, its sloping walls and low ceiling causing them to drop to the floor and crawl along.

They passed through into a chamber and were, at last, able to stand, brushing themselves off and rearranging their creased clothing. They were greeted by a man collecting and crating pieces of pottery and bronze. In the centre of this room was a whitewashed coffin, open and empty.

'Ah, you must be the professor and

his daughter.' The man looked up from where he was carefully packing the antiquities. 'These are going to be logged. They're fragile, see?' He held up a small shard of pottery. 'From a plate — see the fruit design? And here's a canopic jar. Thieves have smashed most of it. The mummy was taken from the coffin, but we have a hand. It's often the case that in the time of thieves, mummies were destroyed along with what were considered worthless artefacts.'

'There's no mummy?' Davis asked, dismayed. 'Then we don't know whose tomb this was.'

The man shook his head. 'Not really, although some pottery has been inscribed on the bottom with the name Amratep. However, this is not as lavish as a royal tomb.'

Davis looked at the shard. Amber took his hand and gave it a reassuring squeeze. 'I'm sure we'll find out who was buried here, Father. The name on the pottery alone must mean that it's important. It's a lead, surely?'

He gave her a watery smile. 'Perhaps; but we're looking for a royal tomb. This pottery could be commemorative, such as we have for coronations today. It isn't enough to say it actually belonged to Amratep. I just hope we haven't come here for nothing.'

When they ascended once again into the heat and dusty dryness, James met them. Amber's heart flipped, as it was now wont to do when she saw him.

'My father is anxious to see what you make of this.' He looked at Amber. 'Miss Davis, Miss Dobson is eager to see you. I think she wishes to ask your opinion on the tent that has been put up for you.'

'The tent is up? How exciting!' Amber tripped off to find Laura and to see how homely the shelter was. She arrived to find that the fabric was strong and of a creamy colour. Inside, Laura had set up two beds, complete with rugs and pillows.

There was much to do on the camp.

Whilst Laura worked at sorting and darning clothes and making the tent snug, Amber begged to be allowed to help crate the antiquities. She was given the task of placing the bronze finds into wooden packing cases. She watched as they were cleaned and logged. They would go to the museum.

Davis was looking at the few really important finds that had been laid aside for him to see. Hayes was clumping behind, mopping his heavy brow with a handkerchief and looking uncomfortable and worried.

The rest of the afternoon was a joy for Amber. She had fulfilled an ambition that had been burning inside her for as long as she could ever remember. Here she was with her beloved father, actually working on an excavation. The joy was made all the greater by tantalising glimpses of James as he walked around the site, notebook in hand. Every so often he would stop and write furiously in his jotter. His golden hair seemed all the brighter, his skin more bronze and firm. Amber could deny it no longer: she was in love with him, and would tell him so.

And later that night as she slid, weary but satisfied, into her camp bed, she realised that the only blot on the perfect day was the fact that she had never actually managed to speak to James. In fact, it was as if he had been avoiding her.

The next day, however, she awoke to find that the happiness that had helped her sleep so soundly was short-lived.

9

Amber and Laura went to savour the breakfast cooked on a roaring fire. They drank cups of milky tea gratefully, and happily devoured the meat and beans cooked by a cheerful man who must have been eighty years old if he were a day.

'My father seems to be sleeping in,' Amber said. They were sitting underneath a makeshift canopy, on a rug placed on the sandy floor and scattered with a myriad of cushions with brightly patterned woven covers.

'The journey is arduous.' Hammed Saidi broke off a sliver of light bread to scoop up some tahini paste. 'I am sure he will join us soon. In fact, I shall go and wake him. We are to clear out the second chamber. I know he wanted to see that.' He rose and made his way to the professor's tent.

Amber sat back against one of the cushions. 'I keep thinking that this must be a dream. I can't believe that I'm actually here.'

'The insect bites won't let me forget,' grumbled Laura, rubbing at her arm where, under her sleeve, there were little red pinpricks that itched.

'Insects are commonplace here,' Amber told her. 'I shall help you put some lotion on in a while. Then perhaps you'd like to see the second chamber with us?'

Laura shuddered. 'I'm afraid I don't relish the idea of clambering through that dark tomb. I'm quite content to sit in the shade and read. Plus, I would like to try and mend the skirt you tore yesterday.'

Amber remembered the small rent in the bottle-green fabric, an accident of catching it on a piece of rock that jutted out from the wall. 'If you're sure, Laura. But I know you'd find it fascinating.'

Laura shuddered again. 'I can assure

you, Miss Amber, I wouldn't.'

Amber was enjoying a second cup of tea when Hammed Saidi returned. His face was creased in a frown, and he looked worried and puzzled.

'Miss Davis,' he said, 'I cannot find your father. In fact, here is a note. He left it on his bed. It seems that he has gone to Siwa Oasis to follow a lead there.'

'Siwa?' Amber took the note and read it. 'There's nothing at Siwa that could possibly help, I'm sure.'

'I will go and ask Mr Hayes if he knows anything about this.'

He returned with Lachlan and James. Lachlan greeted Amber stiffly and looked uncomfortable. 'Mr Saidi tells me that your father has left us.'

'I'm sure he would never have done such a thing,' Amber said.

Hayes read the note. 'This is his own notebook paper, is it not?'

Amber had to agree that it was.

'I'm no expert on archaeology, but this note tells us he's travelled north towards the oases on the west bank.' Hayes shuffled a little. 'It seems plain that he's gone.'

'And has therefore crossed back over the river,' put in James. 'It makes no sense. He would have told someone that he was going.'

Hayes sighed. 'I can only imagine that he was in a hurry to get there.'

'At night?' James was obviously sceptical.

'Mr Hayes,' Amber said, desperate for him to listen, 'I'm convinced that the circumstances aren't what they seem.'

'Miss Davis,' Lachlan snapped back, 'I'm sorry that your father saw fit to leave you in my care. It's irresponsible, especially when I have my own concerns with my son.'

'I must demur, Mr Hayes. Something about this isn't right,' Amber insisted.

'Then follow him. And take James with you.' Hayes stomped off, clouds of dust and sand flying up where he walked.

Amber looked at James with tears in her eyes. 'All along I've known that something was amiss. This whole trip has been dogged somehow.'

James faltered a little, then took her small hand between his own. 'I promise that I will endeavour to help you find your father. I agree wholeheartedly that he wouldn't just up and leave.'

'I'm grateful to you,' Amber sniffed, suddenly filled with the urge to embrace him.

'If you don't mind being with me, then I think we shall take my father's advice and follow the hint given in the note. We have only this one clue — Siwa. It's on the other side of the river. There's a little dock near here — we can find out if he did take a boat across.'

'Excuse me.'

Both Amber and James turned to see Hammed Saidi standing behind them, a nervous look on his face.

'Excuse me,' he repeated, 'but I too am worried about the professor. You are right, I know that he has no leads at the oasis. And I know that he would not just leave. He would need equipment; workers. Besides, he would never go without telling anyone.'

Amber looked relieved. Two people shared her fear. 'Can I see my father's tent?' she asked.

'Of course.' Hammed led them to it.

Upon entering, Amber could see that her father's rucksack had gone, as had his jacket and notebook. Fired by desperation, she began to search though his belongings. It was not long before her hand alighted on something cool and metallic beneath the woollen blanket on his bed. She flung back the cover and gasped. Her father's spectacles! Now she knew that he had not gone anywhere willingly.

She ran out to James, who said grimly, 'Then this confirms our suspicions.' He paused, then announced with determination: 'We shall beg, borrow or steal a seaworthy vessel from the dock and sail across to the other bank. Siwa might be a red herring, but it's all we have. It looks as if your father was taken by force, Amber. Maybe he was made to write the note. Perhaps Siwa is a cryptic message or clue to his whereabouts.'

Just then, Laura rushed up. 'I've just heard that the professor has gone. Oh, Amber! Is it true?'

Amber clutched at Laura's hand. 'Yes. But we're going to try and find him. We must travel back across the Nile.'

'I shall come too,' said Laura, her head high.

'Then that's four of us,' James concluded. He began to outline a plan. Neither Laura nor Amber had any qualms about the journey.

★ ★ ★

James and Hammed helped the ladies to mount the waiting camels. The ride was tense, as all four were lost in their own concerns.

Upon reaching the dock, with its white-sailed boats bobbing gently, Hammed and James went to arrange a boat to take them over to the west bank. There was worrying news when they returned.

'I asked the boatman if he had seen your father.' Hammed bit at his lip. 'He told me that three men came early this morning and took a boat. I asked him to describe these men, and one sounded just like the professor.'

'He went with the two other men?'

Amber looked at Laura, her concern reaching a white heat that burned into her.

'Yes. All three were westerners. The boatman is sure they were all English. The man who I recognised as your father was being helped by the two men.'

Amber swallowed the bile that had risen in her throat. 'Helped him? Why did he need help?'

'The men he was with explained that he had poor sight and was old.'

Amber was sure of it now: her father had been kidnapped. And he had no spectacles. He would be struggling; and knowing him, his thoughts would be of his daughter. She would waste no time in getting to him.

* * *

The sensational landscape of the desert was dotted with oases. Siwa was far north, and it would be a long and hot journey. The boat ride allowed for bunched muscles to relax a little. James and Amber manoeuvred the boat across the water.

By the time they eventually docked, the Nile and its banks had taken on a rose-orange hue, with palm trees black against the dropping red sun. The temperature had fallen, and Amber became aware of how rushed and ill-conceived this expedition was. Their baggage was scant, as most of their belongings had been left at the archaeologists' camp. They had been extremely impulsive in their concern for the professor.

The next part of the journey had to be made on foot. Hammed suggested that while they still had the coolness of the coming evening before the chill of the desert night, they should walk a little more and see if they could reach an oasis in time to set up camp for the night.

'Be careful,' he warned. 'The sand dunes shift all the time, and cannot be used as landmarks.'

They set off, each determined not to let the others down. The trek was difficult. Amber and Laura had sturdy boots, but they were still only of thin leather that was, of course, not designed for such a hike. By the time the chill began to bite and the growing darkness started to envelop them, all four were becoming decidedly disheartened and worried that they'd not be able to find a suitable place for the night.

'I shall go on ahead,' James said eventually. 'I can set up the tents if I find a suitable place. Hammed, you stay with the ladies and help them.'

'No, Mr James — I will go on. I can speak with Bedouin if I come across them, and I know suitable places. I think you should stay with Miss Davis and Miss Dobson.' He walked off, soon swallowed by the dusk and the large, looming sand dunes.

Later, after climbing a few dunes, slipping and stumbling with no real footholds, Amber, Laura and James were met by the sight of fires and the sound of talking. They had reached a Bedouin camp and tree-lined oasis. Hammed was talking to a man, and when he saw his companions, he gestured for them to come over.

'We have been allowed to stay with these good people. But we have a slight concern. There will be a sand storm.'

'What?' his companions all exclaimed together.

Hammed continued, 'This man says that within a day or two, the storm will come.'

'But does that mean it won't be safe for us to travel further?' James asked.

'We are advised to stay here until it passes,' Hammed told them.

'No!' Amber was shocked. What might happen to her father if they were delayed for any length of time? 'We must continue tomorrow.'

'It is not safe,' Hammed explained. 'We may not be able to reach Siwa in time.'

James sat down on the rugs laid out on the sand. 'Let me think. Your father and his abductors had a good head start on us, a few hours. Hammed, did they pass by here?'

Hammed spoke in the Bedouin tongue, then turned to James. 'Yes, earlier today. They were offered shelter too, but refused.'

Hammed and the Bedouin chief had another quick conversation. Hammed shook his head. 'All we know is that they were en route to the Sacred Tombs.'

'Then that's where we must go,'

Amber said. 'Would we be able to reach them now?'

James took her hand and pulled her onto the rug beside him. 'Amber, please. We'll rest, and consider what to do tomorrow.'

'It will take another half day at least to reach the tombs,' Hammed told them. 'If we eat, drink and rest now, we will be able to continue on. That is, if the storm does not blow in.'

Amber had to admit defeat. She ate little and did not want to sleep in the tent. Wrapping herself up in a cloak and some blankets, she sat hunched over her worry and misery, a little way from camp, weeping.

'Amber?' The warm and welcome voice of James reached her through her tears. He was sitting beside her, stroking her hair. 'I know how worried you are, my dear. I only want to do this safely. We'll be of no use to your father if we behave recklessly.'

'Am I to be wise, then?' She sat up, her face stained and streaked with tears, her lovely dark eyes red and sore. 'I told you that I didn't want to be wise.'

'That was when we were discussing falling in love,' he reminded her gently.

'Well, yes. But the same stands now. I wish more than anything to find my father.'

'I promised you that we will, and I'll keep that promise. But to do that, I must be sensible and listen to the Bedouin, who know the desert better than anyone.' His large hand stroked away a tear from her cheek. 'Please don't cry.'

Amber gave an unladylike sniffle, and realised just how close he was to her.

'Talking of falling in love,' James said, 'you never did finish telling me about your beau.'

Amber frowned in incomprehension. 'Sorry?'

'You told my father that there was someone else. You gave that as the reason why you couldn't marry him.'

'There's no one else. What I mean is,

there is, but he doesn't know it.'

'I think you'd be surprised to find that he does.'

It was inevitable that his blond head should dip towards hers and his warm lips meet her own soft, quivering mouth. She was not shocked. She let him kiss her gently, then gave a mewl of disappointment when he broke away.

'We are, it seems, once more alone in each other's company,' James remarked with a soft laugh. 'So now, if you'll allow me — and hoping that we won't have to catch burglars — I'll tell you what I've been waiting to say.'

Amber thought her breath would simply stop. She looked at him with eager curiosity.

'I want to say that I've been unsure how to play this. I never knew how you felt about me, and I've always been wary of your sensibilities. I know that Laura can be a tigress when she looks out for your welfare, and I wanted to save you from feeling embarrassed.

Now, I'm able to see that you feel the same as I do.'

'What way is that?'

'Ah, you tease me now, Miss Amber Davis.' He took her fingertips and brought them to his lips. 'I've fallen. No map, no compass — just me falling in love with you.'

'Then we're both in trouble, because I don't have a map or compass either.'

James laughed and kissed her once more. 'So, once this is over, am I to assume that you'll still be in love with me?'

'Forever.' She smiled through her tears, feeling as if she could do anything now that she knew James loved her.

10

'The storm is certainly heading this way,' said Hammed the next morning. 'But we might be able to make it to Siwa.'

'Please, we must try.' Amber had woken early. Her lips still burned with James's kiss.

'I am not happy about it, but there is a chance that we could manage. It might be a day or two before the storm.'

'Then we have no time to lose.' James began to gather up the small collection of their belongings and bundle them back up. Suddenly a piercing scream startled them.

'Laura!' Amber raced down to the water's edge to find her maid sitting on a rock, holding her leg.

'I've been stung or bitten by something,' she sobbed.

Hammed took a look at her leg, holding it gently. 'Please, Miss Davis, help Miss Dobson to remove her boots and stockings.'

James suddenly called out, 'A scorpion! That must have been what attacked her. That rock must have been its hiding place.'

'Describe it to me,' Hammed said, looking closely at Laura's ankle.

James did, and was relieved when Hammed declared it to be not poisonous. Hammed took a small penknife from his bag. 'Miss Dobson, I am afraid that this will hurt, but you must be brave. If I can clean the wound, you will be all right.'

Amber held Laura as she gritted her teeth and braced herself as the wound was washed and bound, and Hammed carried Laura back to the camp. 'You need to rest. You cannot walk on that leg.'

'But the professor,' Laura groaned. 'I must help you find him.'

The Bedouin chief spoke to Hammed.

'He has some ointment that will take care of your leg. He tells me you are welcome to stay here while we go on. The women here will let you stay in one of their tents. They will care for you. I will care for Mr James and Miss Davis.'

'I can't leave Laura.' Amber was very distressed at her maid's misadventure.

'Miss Amber, please — you all go on,' Laura insisted. 'I simply don't think I can walk yet. It's too painful.' She looked pale, and a light sheen of perspiration glistened on her forehead.

'It would be best to stay here with you, then,' Amber said, helping Laura to get comfortable.

'No. Please find him. I pray that he's safe. Leave me here. I know I'm in good hands.' Laura lay back and gave a ragged sigh. 'I'll be better off resting here.'

James and Hammed left it to Amber to decide what to do. The thought of leaving her maid — no, not just maid, but friend — was very upsetting. But they had to find her father.

Eventually, reassured that Laura was in the safe hands of the camp's womenfolk, Amber told James and Hammed that she wished to set off for the tombs. They had to carry on before they were caught in the sandstorm.

* * *

'The Sacred Tombs.' Hammed pulled his camel to a stop and pointed to limestone cliffs receding into a dip of rock on the smooth, sandy plateau. Hammed had told them that the Sacred Tombs were cut into the rock. They loomed up before them. The party would reach them on foot in an hour or so.

'My word.' James shielded his eyes. 'And you think the professor is in there?'

'There is nothing else for miles.'

The atmosphere of the desert was becoming oppressive. The temperature had shot up and was now becoming almost unbearable, and a south-westerly wind had begun to blow, whipping up fine clouds of sand.

'We must set up camp now,' James advised. 'The storm is starting.'

Pulling a shawl over her head, Amber hunched against the buffeting of the wind. It was so frustrating to be so near to the tombs and possibly her father, only to stop now. But Hammed had said that the men may have decided to shelter in the tombs until the storm had passed.

They reached the crest of a small dune and saw Hammed, standing with something in his hands. He looked up and waved to James and Amber. 'Please come here. I have found something.'

Amber and James scrabbled down to their friend and saw that he was holding a small pouch of hardened leather. 'That is my father's pouch!' Amber exclaimed, taking it from him. It was still full of chisels and brushes. 'My mother gave it to him when he gained his degree. I know he would never have been careless with it. He's been taken by force.'

'But think of this,' James said. 'At least we know that we're on the right track. They're definitely going towards the tombs.'

'We really must set up now,' Hammed advised.

The wind was becoming a tyrant, and the sand was curling up on eddies of hot air. The men began to pitch the tents.

'It is going to be difficult to hold these down,' said Hammed, his voice snatched by the wind. 'We need to find some big rocks to help tether them.'

'We could go and find some while Amber shelters in this tent.' James placed the bundles of luggage inside. 'Try to tether it as best you can,' he told her. 'The sand alone won't hold it — perhaps you should put these bags down to hold it steady. We won't be long.'

'Please be careful,' Amber pleaded.

'Take care, my darling, and stay inside.' James took her hand and kissed it.

*　★　★

When the two men had gone, Amber closed the door of the tent and sat inside. She knew that they would not be long, if they could help it. Outside, the hot wind pulled at the tent, and sand blustered in under the fabric.

She looked at her little silver watch and groaned. Sand must have worked its way inside, because it had stopped. She had no idea what time it was and would not know how long James and Hammed had been gone.

She took her father's spectacles from the red leather case and held the cold glass and metal. Tears slipped unbidden down her cheeks, making them sore; for the sharp, tiny grains of sand had scraped them as they had swirled up around her.

She opened one of the ties of the tent door in order to peep out, but was met only by a cloud of sand. It blew into her eyes and, squealing, she retied the strings quickly.

Blinded by the sand and shaky with nerves, she stumbled back onto the makeshift bed. The water canteen she found by groping about, but she was too worried about using precious water to completely clear all the grains from her eyes. Using as little liquid as she could, she rinsed until she could see again. But her eyes smarted. She let them water; it would clear the remaining particles of sand.

Now her mind was bursting with worry. James and Hammed were stuck out in the terrible storm. What would happen to them if she had suffered with just one small blast of sandy wind?

It was only as she lay back on the rugs that she realised that she was no longer holding the precious spectacles. She wiped her hand over her stinging eyes and began moving the rugs and bags, but to no avail. The spectacles had disappeared. She even dug a little in the sandy floor beneath the blankets with bare hands; her fingers did not alight on them.

'Where are they?' she muttered, furiously casting aside rugs and her own small sackcloth bag. Her father would need them; she had to find them. She sat back on her heels. 'Think, Amber, think. They can't possibly be far. You haven't gone anywhere.'

Then, to her horror, it struck her that she had had them whilst opening the tent door. The spectacles must be outside — she must have dropped them in her shock at being hit by the blast of sand! She could not risk going back into the storm.

She really wanted to doze, but felt compelled to stay awake in order to wait for James and Hammed. However, the adventures she had endured made her tired, and she found her sore eyes becoming heavy; her head simply wanted to rest against the rug. She fell asleep.

★ ★ ★

When she awoke, it took a few moments to work out where she was.

151

When her tired, fuzzy mind eventually remembered, two things struck her. First, it was darker. Second, the sound of the gale and the sand blowing in under the tent had stopped.

Cautiously, she opened one of the ties and peeked out. The storm had gone. The stars were bright dots, the stones and cliffs silver. The humps of the dunes stood inky against the darkening sky. There was no sign of either James or Hammed Saidi.

Amber crawled out of the tent and stood up, grateful to stretch her long legs and sore back. She stepped with care, mindful of her father's spectacles. She crouched down and began to feel around for them, clawing at the small sand drifts. So immersed in her task was she that when she heard a soft, muffled footfall behind her, she could not later say how long she had not been alone.

Her immediate thought was that James and Hammed had returned. She spun round, then gasped. It was

Stamford Baxter and another smaller, stockier man. Their shaded silhouettes told her that these were the men she had seen breaking into the Grand Plaza Hotel.

Scrambling up, her foot hit something. Looking down, she saw the arm of her father's spectacles sticking out from the sand. She scooped them up. Baxter made a grab for her.

Amber ran, her breath hot and stinging her lungs. The air was close, still a little sandy. She stumbled and tripped, calling for James.

She could hear thumping behind her and turned and screamed. Baxter and his associate had camels! That second of realisation caused her to let out a sob of despair. Who could outrun a camel in the desert?

She was hauled up onto Baxter's camel, held closely and painfully in one arm, while he clutched the reins with the other.

'You and your father have led us a merry dance,' Baxter said. 'Your father was the real target, but since you're here too and obviously know the score, you might as well come with us.'

'Is my father all right?' Amber willed her breathing to be steady. She could not allow herself to panic.

'Oh, a little tied up at the moment,' sneered the small man.

'I assume you're taking me to him?' The jogging of the camel was beginning to give her a headache. She could see little now. Where was James? It seemed that her worst fear was realised. He and Hammed could not possibly have survived the gusts and gales of the sandstorm.

The camels slowed to a trot and then a wobbly gait. They had reached the Sacred Tombs. Amber was slung down off the animal and had a painful, bruising fall. Baxter grabbed her and took hold of her long hair, which had worked loose.

'Let's go on a little climb.'

Amber gasped. The rock face was roughened and much eroded in places, but it was still steep, and the fall into the rocky basin below would be fatal. She was hauled and pushed up the rock face. Small, uneven steps had been crudely carved into the sides. She clung to the rock with her nails and hauled herself, with the rough help of her two abductors, up onto a narrow ledge.

Panting, the stocky man said, 'Professor, we have someone to visit you.' He pushed Amber inside a small tomb, cut deep in the stone.

'Father?'

'Amber?' His voice had come from the dense shadows cast by the flickering flame of a candle. 'I'm here, I'm all right, but they've tied me up.'

'And a good job, too.' Baxter pulled Amber's slender arms together and tied her wrists tightly with an itchy rope. Then he tied her ankles. The twine bit into her delicate flesh. 'You two can wait here until morning. Then we'll consider what to do with you. I imagine we'll get a few camels for that pretty maid.' The two men sneered.

'We shall be in the apartment below,' the stocky bulldog of a man said sarcastically.

Amber's eyes became used to the shadows and weird light thrown by the candles. She could see the figure of her father sitting against the wall.

'Oh, thank goodness you're alive,' Amber said. 'I'm afraid I had your spectacles, but I lost them again when those brutes hauled me onto their camels.'

'Are you hurt, Amber?'

'A little sore, but I'll live.' She shuffled over and sank against him. 'I have no idea where James and Hammed are, though. Oh Father, I'm so frightened that James might be dead!'

'Pardon? Will you explain what's been going on? How is it that you've found me?'

She began to tell him of the discovery of his disappearance and the subsequent chase across the river and the desert. Her father listened, wide-eyed, his face blanching when she recounted

Laura's scorpion disaster. It was only when she told her father that James and Hammed were missing that she found her voice catching in her throat. The horror of losing James made her lean against her father and weep.

When Amber had exhausted her tears, the professor let out a heavy breath. 'Well, I'll never underestimate your tenacity, my dear. You are a credit to me. However, if you ever try anything as irresponsible again, I shall be so cross — '

'I may be in danger here, but at least I've found you.'

'The point is Amber, that you've put yourself in this situation. I dread to think what will happen. It's bad enough having to worry about myself, but now I have my headstrong daughter to add to my concern. What father was ever so sorely tried?'

Amber leant over and kissed his cheek. 'I am a trial to you, but you wouldn't have it any other way.'

'I suppose not.' Davis smiled gently

at her. Then the smile faded and he looked grave. 'But I meant what I said; I'm very worried about what will happen to us. I don't even know why I am here, Amber.'

She tried to be reassuring. 'Look at the positives. There are now two of us. At least neither of us is alone.' James would not want her dwelling on the black side of things.

11

Stones were being disturbed as some-one climbed the rough cut-away steps. Light filtered in through the narrow entrance, sending a ray of sun in to splash on the wall.

'Amber?' The voice was a hiss, but wonderfully familiar. 'She must be near here; she has to be. The spectacles and pouch were here.'

'She must have dropped them.'

'James? Hammed?' Amber jolted her father awake with her bound hands. 'James and Hammed Saidi are alive!'

Davis shook himself out of his sleep.

'Amber, can you hear me?'

The voices were faint, coming from below the tomb in which Amber and her father were held captive. The deep chamber made it almost impossible for Amber to make her voice carry. She called again, but got no reaction that told her she'd been heard.

'Father, what shall we do? They can't hear us.'

Davis considered the problem. 'We could perhaps shuffle to the entrance and call or drop something from the doorway.'

'I'll go.' Amber looked around and her gaze fell on the candle. It had petered out, but she had an idea. She shuffled slowly towards it. Curling and contorting her slender frame, she managed to grip it in her teeth, grimacing at the taste of the wax, but determined in her quest.

'Amber, be careful,' warned her father.

She shuffled and scraped along on her bottom, wincing as sharp stones dug and cut. She could only just hear James and Hammed calling. They were moving away from the tomb, probably round to the other face. All would be lost if they left before she had carried out her plan.

She reached the entrance, sore and

bruised. There she dropped the candle, along with a few loose stones, and pushed them out of the tomb with her fettered feet.

She was gratified at the clatter they made as they fell. And her heart beat faster when she heard James's and Hammed's voices become closer and closer. She called and almost swooned with relief when she was answered. It was only a few moments before the face of James Hayes looked through the narrow entrance.

'Well done!' he said, clambering into the tomb, followed by a panting Hammed. 'Is your father here? Are you hurt?'

'I'm a little sore,' Amber admitted, 'but apart from that, my father and I are both well.'

'Good, good.'

'James?' she began.

'Yes, my darling?'

She held out her wrists. 'If you wouldn't mind.'

'Oh yes, of course.' He untied her

wrists and she set herself to untying the rope round her ankles.

'Tell me where you've been,' Amber said. 'I thought something dreadful had happened to you.' She began to rub her circulation back into order and soothe the ache and sting of the twine. While she massaged her arms and legs, Hammed went to help the professor, and James told her how they had sheltered by a rocky outcrop, putting their coats over their heads and blocking as much sand as they could with boulders.

'We heard the men ride past,' James said. 'They were rushing to get to the tombs. They mentioned your father. We saw you being taken, and had to wait until the kidnappers were out of sight and earshot before we could rescue you.'

'Thank goodness you did.'

'Amber, if I were to kiss you again, would that be too much?'

She shook her head and smiled shyly. 'I could cope.'

Their lips met, and she clung to James, her body filled with the sensation that she was melting and falling into some deep, wonderful place.

By the time Hammed returned with the professor, Amber and James were peering out of the tomb entrance. 'The camels are still there,' Amber said. 'The kidnappers said they were staying here too.'

'And so they are. But don't worry, we've managed to take care of that little problem. They are at this moment somewhat restricted by the reins of their own chargers.'

'Ah, so the camels came in useful then,' Davis said.

'And will do so again. They're our mounts for today. Miss Davis, Professor Davis, let's climb back down and get back to the oasis. Miss Dobson will be worried sick.'

The professor's face became as pallid as the candle Amber had pushed from the tomb. 'Do you think she'll be all right?'

'I am sure she's more worried about you two, despite her sore leg. But apart from those concerns,' James added with a grin, 'I should imagine she's fine and dandy. Now, if it's all the same, can we get going? The camels aren't tethered now, and I for one don't fancy the idea of walking all the way back again. Let's get them before they start trekking. Oh, by the way, Professor Davis, here are your spectacles and tool pouch.'

★ ★ ★

The party made their way back to the camp, where they parted ways with a smiling Hammed, who extracted a promise from the professor to return for a somewhat less exciting stay in the near future. Amber's head was still spinning with all that had happened and she found herself just wanting to sleep, safely snuggled into the soft, brightly coloured cushions in the coolness of the tent.

The first person Amber recognised at

the camp was Laura, who was sitting beneath the shade of a makeshift veranda, her leg held steady by a cushion beneath it.

'Laura!' Amber hugged her maid close. 'How are you? I can't tell you what adventures we've had.'

'My leg is healing well, and I'm so very relieved to see you all safe.'

Davis shyly stepped forward. 'Laura, from what Amber tells me, you were a stalwart companion on this reckless adventure. I only hope you don't hold it against us that you were hurt.'

Laura struggled to her feet and limped to the professor. 'I certainly don't.'

Amber gave James a meaningful look as her father coyly took Laura in his arms and hugged her. James winked and blew Amber a cheeky kiss.

'Am I to take it, Father, that you and Laura are pleased to be reunited?' Amber asked impertinently, her eyes bright with the hope that this was so.

'We were going to wait and tell you

when we returned to England, but that seems rather tame now.' Davis took Laura's hand and beamed. 'Laura has decided to be foolhardy enough to consent to be my wife.'

Amber shrieked with joy and threw herself at her father and future stepmother, embracing them in a tight and excited hug.

'Congratulations, Professor, Miss Dobson.' James stood back, allowing the new family to celebrate together.

When the party eventually arrived at the excavation site, they were given a shock. Hayes had been found to be shipping the crates of antiquities to the address of a confederate, who was disposing of them. He'd admitted trying to hide the evidence of an important site. After further questioning, he had also admitted dogging the professor and trying to have him removed until the site was cleared and there was no more evidence to show what the site was.

'I'm glad that he'll pay for all this,'

James said, 'even though he is my father.'

The only blot on the horizon was the fact that another Egyptologist had looked at the artefacts. He had declared them to be from the tomb of Ankhra, not Amratep. Ankhra's mummy had not been found, presumably taken by devotees and hidden away to save it from being violated by tomb robbers. Davis was, of course, disappointed at not having found the princess's tomb, but vowed to continue his search for the solution to the mystery.

On the journey back to Cairo, the party stopped for a view of Giza at dusk. Amber slipped off alone to gaze at the huge pyramids, first rosy, then silver in the falling light, now unimpeded by the brick walls and litter-filled yards of her arrival. This was what she had imagined. This was how they should be seen.

'Amber? I've done it again — found you alone.'

'I don't feel alone, not with such

monuments as chaperones,' Amber said, not able to take her eyes from the structures that dominated the view.

'True. This really is a romantic place.'

'I hope my father and Laura are enjoying the romance, then.'

'You two ladies will have much to discuss. I only hope you won't argue over who has which flowers or who wears what veil.'

Amber frowned. 'Pardon?'

'Well, since you're both to be married.'

With her mouth suddenly dry as powder, Amber asked, 'Am I to be married? I haven't been informed of the fact.'

'Ah,' James breathed dramatically. He scratched his head and pursed his lips in thought. 'Ah. Well . . . wait. Yes, I see what's happened. In all the excitement of having to rescue you and your father, it must have slipped my mind to ask you if you would do me the honour of being my wife.'

'Slipped your mind?'

168

'Only for a tiny, brief moment.' He grinned.

'I suppose that now that you've put me on the spot, I'd better accept, had I not?' Amber smiled back at him.

'I don't know about Egypt being the 'gift of the Nile',' said James, taking his love into his arms. 'I think that you've been the best present I've ever been lucky enough to have.'

We do hope that you have enjoyed reading this large print book.

Did you know that all of our titles are available for purchase?

We publish a wide range of high quality large print books including:
Romances, Mysteries, Classics
General Fiction
Non Fiction and Westerns

Special interest titles available in large print are:
The Little Oxford Dictionary
Music Book, Song Book
Hymn Book, Service Book

Also available from us courtesy of Oxford University Press:
Young Readers' Dictionary
(large print edition)
Young Readers' Thesaurus
(large print edition)

For further information or a free brochure, please contact us at:
Ulverscroft Large Print Books Ltd.,
The Green, Bradgate Road, Anstey,
Leicester, LE7 7FU, England.
Tel: (00 44) **0116 236 4325**
Fax: (00 44) **0116 234 0205**